HOW LONG BEFORE ANOTHER GUNMAN CAME TO CHALLENGE HIM?

"Smith!"

Slocum turned back toward the house.

The kid was holding his Colt and his rifle. "Here you go, Reb. Don't shoot yourself in the foot."

Slocum took his weapons, inspecting them carefully.

"I didn't do anything," the kid said. "Don't you trust me?"

Slocum's eyes were green slits in the sun. "Tell me you wouldn't like to see me dead."

"I would. But only if I'm shootin' you, Smith. Smith? That's a pretty common name."

"What of it?"

The kid grinned. "That's my name, too. Jimmy Smith."

Slocum turned away, heading for the stable.

"See you on Saturday night," the kid called.

Slocum kept walking. He wasn't afraid of the kid. But he still wanted to get the hell away from the Cooper Cattle Company.

OTHER BOOKS BY JAKE LOGAN

JAKE LOGAN

SLOCUM'S STANDOFF

BERKLEY BOOKS, NEW YORK

SLOCUM'S STANDOFF

A Berkley Book / published by arrangement with
the author

PRINTING HISTORY
Berkley edition / November 1991

ISBN: 0-425-13037-1

PRINTED IN THE UNITED STATES OF AMERICA

10 9 8 7 6 5 4 3 2 1

This book is dedicated to Kevin Simm

SLOCUM'S
STANDOFF

1

John Slocum cursed the summer heat. The sun beat down on his faded, wide-brimmed hat, which barely provided enough shade for his piercing green eyes.

Slocum's brain was addled by the wretched, unrelenting heat. He knew he had headed north, after that trouble in Raton, but he had turned east somewhere on the arid plain. Now he was totally lost. He was probably close to Texas or Oklahoma, but he wasn't really sure.

Sweat poured out of him. Slocum nursed a swallow from the half-empty canteen. He dismounted to give his sorrel gelding a drink.

He had to find more water soon. The gelding had to do more than just wet its whistle. It had to drink deeply and rest in some shade.

Slocum could have used some shade himself. It had been almost a week since he had his last drop of whiskey. He hadn't had a cigarette in two days, since he had run out of tobacco.

He needed a town. Any town.

He flexed his shoulders. The heat kept him fairly limber, but there was still stiffness in his muscles. Dust covered him in a white sheet.

He gazed toward the wavy lines of heat that rose from the plain. It was going to be tough. He had to take it easy with the sorrel.

Slocum sighed. His mind went back to another sunny day in Georgia, when the Yankee carpetbaggers had cheated him out of everything that had been his life. He had run from the South.

He had been running ever since. There had been trouble on the way. Some towns had posters on Slocum. In most cases the price on his head wasn't high, but it was still a price.

Slocum kept moving on. He would always buy a new horse, ride on to the next town, straight into more trouble. Running always seemed better than staying.

The horse snorted and pricked his ears.

Slocum looked up.

Dust rose on the plain. A rider was coming straight toward him.

Slocum's hand dropped to the Colt. 36 on his side.

The rider reined up when he saw Slocum. He tipped his hat.

Slocum eased his hand away from the pistol.

"Howdy," the rider said, casting his eyes to the sky. "Somethin' of a scorcher, ain't it?"

Slocum nodded. "You coming from a town?"

The rider shrugged. "If you're lookin' for a town, Helltown is that way."

"Helltown?"

"Keep going," the rider warned him. "You'll see."

The rider spurred his mount and dust rose behind him on the dry plain.

Slocum shook his head. "Helltown?"

He gazed through the heat waves on the plain after the rider. Some men were just like that. They had to be sour to a drifter.

Slocum mounted up again.

The sorrel started to walk. It was a strong animal. Slocum wanted to get it watered and give it some rest.

He had plenty of money in his pocket. He had been paid to get out of Raton. It was better than being chased out.

He could make deals with money in his pocket. He could pay a smith to let him sleep in a barn loft if the town had a stable—if there really was a town ahead of him.

Helltown.

The shapes appeared between the heat lines on the horizon. Slocum saw the brown structures and the lone street. It was an ugly, heat-baked place, but it looked beautiful to Slocum.

He was sure he had never been to this town before. There probably wouldn't be any wanted posters on him. He could rest for a couple of days.

Two men gawked at Slocum as he rode past the general store. There was also a saloon and a stage stop.

The stable was on the other side of the street, at the far edge of the dusty town.

Slocum dismounted in front of the barn doors.

A dark-haired man came toward Slocum. "Nice sorrel," the liveryman said. "You wouldn't want to sell him, would you?"

Slocum frowned at him. "Sell?"

"Yeah, I'm always looking for horses. This drought has killed a lot of animals. Name's Ray, Ray Thornton."

Slocum shook hands with the brawny smith. Thornton was a rugged-looking man with broad shoulders and thick arms. He did not look like someone from *Helltown*.

"I might sell him," Slocum said. "But I don't know how long I'll be in town."

Thornton smiled. "You sound like a rebel, sir."

Slocum shot a wary glance at the man. Sometimes his Southern accent got him into trouble. There were still plenty of men around who wanted to fight the war all over again.

"I hail from Louisiana myself," the smithy said. "Always glad to meet a fellow son of Dixie."

Slocum nodded. "Where am I, Thornton?"

"Elkhart, Oklahoma, sir. Cattle country mostly around here. We're right on the Texas border. Course, this drought keeps up much longer, we might have to find something else to ranch."

"How much to stable the gelding?" Slocum asked.

Thornton shrugged. "You let me take him, we'll settle up later."

Slocum was agreeable. "I need a place to sleep, too. And maybe a bath if you got one."

"Take the loft," Thornton replied. "And there's a pump and bucket out back. No tub. Take it easy on the water. We got this drought."

Slocum nodded.

He went through the stable, emerging into a backyard.

The pump emptied cool water into his hands. He washed his face and then drank for a long time. His belly cramped for a minute, but he was all right.

Slocum washed his shirt and then put it back on wet. It would dry quickly in the heat. The coolness felt good against his skin.

He dusted off his jeans and then reached into his pocket.

The wad of money filled his hand. He had scrip and gold. The man had paid him well to get out of Raton. Easy money.

Slocum peeled off several bills. He wanted a drink and some food.

Back inside the livery, Slocum saw that Thornton had already begun to rub down the sorrel.

"Give you forty dollars for him," Thornton said.

Slocum handed him three dollars. "Here, you take this for the first two days and we'll talk about it later."

Thornton accepted the money. "Thanks, stranger. You got a name?"

"John."

"That'll do, John."

"Food," Slocum said. "Where can I find some?"

"Saloon serves a free lunch if you drink," Thornton replied. "I don't drink myself, so I just make a pot of meat and potatoes."

"I'll take the free lunch," Slocum replied.

Slocum stepped up onto the wooden stoop and pushed through the swinging doors of the saloon.

The two men on the porch of the general store took note of his entrance.

"You think *she* hired him?" one man asked.

"He has the look," the other replied. "That gun was hanging pretty low on his hip."

"Maybe I oughta tell the boss."

"If you don't tell him, somebody else will."

"Yeah. And if he is a hired gun, they'll want to get rid of him as soon as possible."

"Get rid of him or hire him."

"I wonder when the sheriff'll be back?"

"Best not to worry about it until the trouble starts."

Slocum was surprised by the saloon. He had expected a run-down, slapdash barroom with overturned spittoons and watered whiskey. But the place was bright and colorful. There was a huge mirror behind the polished bar and a felt-covered gaming table.

A slick-looking man shuffled cards at the table. "Welcome, stranger. Jensen's the name. Tyler Jensen. I can deal faro, blackjack, poker. You care to make a wager?"

Slocum shook his head.

The gambler shrugged. "Suit yourself."

Slocum bellied up to the bar. There was sliced meat, bread, and onions on a tray. He took a piece of the meat.

"Gotta pay for drinks," said a fat-faced bartender.

"I got money," Slocum replied.

The bartender gaped at his wad.

Slocum put a five-dollar gold piece on the counter. "I want all the beer that this will buy and a bottle of whiskey, too."

"Sorry," the bartender said. "I didn't mean to—"

Slocum put the piece of meat between two slices of bread without replying.

The bartender set a bottle of red-eye in front of him.

Slocum drank straight from the bottle. He ate until the lunch platter was empty. The bartender brought more, including some peppers and sweet relish. Slocum finished eating and then bought some cheap tobacco to roll a smoke.

Jensen, the gambler, slid next to Slocum. "Shame to watch a man drink alone. Mind if I take a—"

Slocum pushed the bottle toward the man and grabbed a warm mug of beer for himself. After he emptied the mug, he asked the bartender to pour him another.

Jensen threw back a shot. "Mind if I have one more?"

Slocum grabbed the bottle. He took a long swig. The whiskey was smooth. He gave the bottle back to Jensen.

"Thank you," the gambler replied. "You sure you don't want to sit down at the table for—"

"Save it for the tinhorns," Slocum told him. "I'm no cowpoke looking to blow my wages in one turn of the cards."

"Not even a hand of blackjack?"

"You got my whiskey," Slocum said. "What else do you want?"

"I'll have you know I run a clean game!"

"Sure you do," Slocum said. "You separate fools from their money. I'm no fool."

"I earn a living like anyone else," Jensen insisted. "But I'll have you know that I don't make enough from that gaming table to pay for my dinner."

"Yeah? Then why do you do it?"

"My salary is paid by the owner of this saloon, a Mr. H. L. Cooper of the Cooper Cattle Company. He likes to enjoy a hand of poker with the other ranchers in this area, so he makes it worth my while to stay around."

Slocum chortled. "Then go take *his* money."

"Are you working for Mr. Cooper?" Jensen asked.

"Not yet," Slocum replied.

He wanted to look for work as soon as possible. He hadn't worked in a while. And the wad of money would last longer if he was earning a wage.

"Is Mr. Cooper hiring?" Slocum asked.

Jensen sighed. "I doubt it. The drought has everyone in a dither. I haven't made five dollars this week."

The bartender looked at Slocum. "Another beer?"

The tall, green-eyed rebel nodded. "And one for the card jockey."

"Thank you," Jensen said.

"Why don't you take it back over to your table and leave me be?" Slocum told him.

"Fine by me," the gambler replied. "Can't argue with a man who wants to be alone. You know where to find me if you want to play a few hands."

He left with the beer, returning to the felt table.

Slocum looked at his own reflection in the huge mirror. His face was gaunt and sallow. He barely recognized himself.

"Have another sandwich," the bartender urged.

Slocum's belly was full. "I'll settle for some information."

"I don't know nothing, mister."

"Tell me what I ask, and you can keep the change from that gold piece."

"Sure. What do you want to know?"

"This Cooper. Is he the big man in this town?"

"Yeah, he's the big cheese. Pays the sheriff and most of the others around here. You lookin' for work?"

"Maybe. But the gambler said Cooper isn't taking on hands."

"That depends," the bartender said. "Can you use a gun?"

Slocum's eyes narrowed. "Sometimes I can."

"Then Cooper might hire you. Want to know why he needs guns?"

Slocum shook his head. "No. If there's trouble here, I won't be around long enough to care."

"Then you better move on, stranger."

Slocum eyed the fat-faced man. "Met a rider on the trail. Called this place Helltown."

"Good name for it," the bartender replied. "I'll tell you what it's all about, if you want."

"I said no."

Slocum had his own troubles. He didn't need other people's troubles, too. He decided to steer clear of Elkhart.

He could sleep one night in the stable, then move on the next day.

He would take the bottle with him and leave the bar. The whiskey would help him to fall asleep.

"More beer?" the bartender asked.

Slocum shook his head. He felt tired and decided to go back to the stable and have a nap.

As he turned, the gambler smiled at him. "Sure you don't want to play a hand of faro?"

"I told you I don't—"

Slocum froze in his tracks. He noticed the woman standing behind Jensen. She had brown eyes and dark hair, and she was dressed elegantly in the latest Eastern fashions.

She smiled at Slocum.

He nodded.

She was so damned beautiful.

Jensen grinned. "Well, stranger, I think we've finally found something that you're interested in!"

2

The woman moved from behind the gambler. She took Slocum's arm. "I'm Belle. Would you like to sit down and play cards?"

"I'm not in the mood for cards," Slocum replied.

Belle laughed girlishly. Her bosom jiggled slightly. Slocum could smell her perfume.

Something told him that she was trouble, but he didn't care. The perfume had him.

"Well," she said, "sit down anyway. Maybe we can have a few drinks together. Mr. Jensen and I are good company, at least that's what I've been told."

Slocum sat down with his bottle.

Jensen turned the cards in front of him.

Belle sat down next to Slocum. "Just let him deal you a few hands," she said. "You don't have to bet."

Jensen dealt a perfect blackjack hand to Slocum. "See there, stranger, you're lucky. Give it a try."

But Slocum refused to bet. He just kept his eyes on the woman. She was beautiful and charming, a real lady.

"It's Saturday night," Belle went on. "The cowboys will be here soon. It takes them a while to ride into town from the ranches."

"Ranches?" Slocum said. "I thought there was only one ranch in these parts, owned by a man named Cooper."

"Why, no," Belle started.

Then she caught the look on Jensen's face. He was glaring at her. The look told her to keep her mouth shut.

9

Belle changed the subject. "Would I be impolite if I asked your name, sir?"

"John."

"Just John?"

Slocum nodded. "That's it."

She laughed. "Oh my, another man who doesn't want anyone to know his last name. I swear, since I came West I haven't met a single man who wants me to know his last name."

"Maybe he's wanted around here," Jensen said.

Slocum glared at him. "Don't bet on it."

Jensen shrugged. "Hey, don't take it wrong, John. I was just having a little fun."

"Oh, yeah," Belle rejoined. "Mr. Jensen is full of fun. Why, he's the most fun man in this town."

Slocum knew there was a connection between the girl and the gambler. Was the rich rancher also paying to have the woman at his beck and call? He didn't care very much. He just wanted a shot at her. She would probably want to charge him, but that made no difference to him.

Slocum's eyes kept straying to the dark canyon between her breasts. She was too pretty to be a dance hall girl. The rancher must be paying her.

Suddenly, Jensen lifted a wad of money and put it on the table. "Just sit there," he told Slocum. "Put up a dollar, and I'll see that you win every hand."

Slocum frowned. "What the devil—"

Belle put a finger to her lips. "Shh."

Slocum heard a commotion behind him as the Saturday night cowboys piled into the saloon. Their hands were thick with their pay. They wanted whiskey.

Then somebody noticed the gaming table. "Hey, let's play blackjack."

Jensen smiled as the tables filled up. "It's a fair game, boys."

One of the trail hands looked at Belle. "Why hello, pretty lady."

Belle giggled, taking Slocum's hand. "Sorry, boys. I'm taken tonight. My friend John just dropped into town."

Slocum did not smile. He watched the others, who also gave up on Belle. They wanted to play cards for a while.

Jensen's narrow eyes had fallen on Slocum. "You in, John?"

Slocum put a silver dollar in front of him. "For one hand," the tall rebel replied. "I'll see how it goes."

Jensen shuffled the cards. He dealt blackjack to Slocum again.

"John's a winner," Jensen said and paid off the bet.

Two of the other hands had won as well.

Belle put her head on Slocum's shoulder. "I just know my Johnny's going to be lucky."

The game got hotter. Slocum kept betting a dollar on every hand, and Jensen dealt him winning cards. But what the gambler paid to Slocum, he took tenfold from the others.

"I'm busted."

"Me, too."

"Got just enough left for a bottle."

"Hey, let's get liquored up."

The table emptied.

Jensen slipped his winnings into his pocket. "Never count it at the table," he said.

Slocum sighed. "Here, take this back, Jensen."

He pushed everything but his original dollar toward the gambler.

Jensen frowned. "But I—"

"You got your money," Slocum said. "I can't take what I haven't won fair and square."

Jensen smiled and raked the money toward him. "Well, you are a real Southern gentleman. Mind sitting here for the next bunch of cowboys?"

Slocum looked at Belle. He figured it was do or die. She was probably just stringing him along so Jensen could use him as a shill.

"I was wondering if the lady might like to have a drink," Slocum said. "In private."

Belle tried to blush, but she couldn't quite pull it off. "My, my, John, you sure don't beat around the bush."

"Y'all don't either," the tall man replied. "Well, I reckon

I'll have to take my bottle and go. It's already dark outside.
I need some shut-eye."

Slocum started to get up.

"Don't go," Belle said. "Please."

Slocum looked at her. "You'll keep me here all night. Then
I won't get what I was staying for."

Jensen glared at him. "You don't have to talk like that."

Slocum kept his eyes on the woman. "I apologize to the
lady. But I'd best be on my way."

She grabbed him again. "No."

Slocum sighed. "Ma'am, I—"

She leaned closer and whispered into his ear. "You help
Mr. Jensen with the cowboys, and I'll give you anything
you want." She knew exactly what to say to keep him at
the table.

Slocum took another drink of the red-eye. The bottle was
almost empty. He had Belle go buy him another one.

He looked at the gambler. "How much is she gonna cost
me, Jensen?"

"Don't worry, you'll earn it."

Belle came back with the bottle.

Slocum drank again.

His head was on fire. He wasn't falling down drunk, but
he wasn't sober, either. The woman had done it to him. That
perfume had gotten his blood flowing.

The double doors swung open again.

More boots pounded the barroom floor.

Slocum looked up, expecting to see more gullible cowboys.
Instead, he saw a man with a Winchester.

The rifleman's eyes scanned the barroom.

Jensen grabbed his cards and his money. "I'm getting out
of here."

Slocum expected Belle to leave, too, but she only sat there,
watching the scene unfold.

The rifleman's face broke into a hateful scowl. "Kid! Look
at me, Kid!"

A young, sandy-haired wrangler turned to face him.

"I don't like the way you talked to my daughter!" the
rifleman cried. "If you—"

The young wrangler did not waste any time. He went for his weapon. The pistol exploded, and the rifleman dropped down on one knee.

The wrangler took aim again.

Slocum drew his Colt and shot the pistol out of the young man's hand. It had been a reflex. Slocum could not watch the kid shoot another man who wasn't even trying to fight back. Slocum knew it was a mistake as soon as he fired the shot.

The kid danced around holding his wrist.

Slocum tensed, expecting others to draw on him, but no guns flashed under the dim oil lamps of the saloon.

Slocum moved to help the rifleman. As he touched the man's shoulder, the rifleman fell to the floor.

No one moved to help him, either.

The bullet had entered his shoulder, and blood poured from the hole. Slocum knew he should have stayed out of it. What if the law came in and saw him with a smoking Colt?

He glanced at Belle. "You got a doctor in this town?"

She shook her head.

Before he could say anything else, a young woman burst through the doors of the saloon.

She had blond hair and a pretty face. She knelt next to the fallen man. Tears filled her blue eyes.

"I told you to leave him alone, Father! Help us. Somebody please help us."

At the girl's request, several of the hands moved to lift the man from the floor.

Her blue eyes fell on Slocum for a moment. Then she turned to leave, taking her father with her.

Slocum looked at the kid. The bartender had started to bandage his hand. Slocum wondered why the others had not defended him.

The kid glared at Slocum. "You're gonna pay for this."

Slocum grabbed his bottle and strode out of the saloon in disgust—with himself and with the whole situation. He hadn't been in Elkhart for a whole day, and he had already gotten himself into trouble. Why had he drawn on the man? It wasn't his problem.

As he went outside into the hot air, he heard a wagon

rolling away. Dust stirred in the darkness. It was going to be a hot, gritty night.

He headed toward the stable, wondering if it might just be better to ride on. He had plenty of money left. His head was a little thick from the drink, but he was able to ride.

Thornton, the liveryman, was still at his forge. "Heard some shooting over at the saloon."

"I had to plug this kid," Slocum replied.

Thornton frowned. "Sandy-haired punk?"

Slocum nodded. "Know him?"

"They call him the Cimarron Kid," Thornton replied. "You got off a shot against him. You must be fast. You're still alive."

Slocum sighed. He uncorked the bottle. His throat burned as the red-eye went down.

"Yeah, that kid is trouble," Thornton went on. "I bet nobody even tried to help him when you started shooting."

"He drew on another man," Slocum replied. "Plugged him and then was gonna shoot him while he was down."

"Not right," Thornton agreed.

Slocum took another nip of the red-eye. It nipped him back. His head reeled. He rolled another cigarette and lit it.

"You okay, John?" Thornton asked.

Slocum nodded. "Nobody wanted to help that kid."

"No, he's kind of a sore spot around here. Nobody likes him, but they leave him alone."

"What about the sheriff?"

Thornton shrugged. "He takes orders from Mr. Cooper. If Cooper says to leave the kid alone, he leaves him alone."

Slocum gazed into the smithy's fire. The flames seemed to form images before his eyes.

"Who'd the kid shoot?" Thornton asked.

Slocum shrugged. "Some older man. His daughter came and got him. They rode off in a wagon."

"That'd be the Wheelers," Thornton replied. "From over at the Lazy River C. There's all kinds of bad blood between the Wheelers and Cooper. If you want to—"

Slocum waved it off. "Don't tell me any more, Thornton. I don't want to know. I'm leaving first thing in the morning."

"Smart move," Thornton replied. "I'd leave, too, if I didn't own this stable."

Slocum staggered toward the ladder that rose to the loft. "John?"

He turned to face Thornton.

"Well," the smith said, "I was just wondering if you were going to sell me that sorrel."

"What do you think?" Slocum said.

Thornton shook his head. "I think you want a good animal to get you out of here."

Slocum climbed the ladder. He almost lost his balance once, but then he swung over onto the loft.

The dry hay smelled sweet. He leaned back on the soft cushion. It reminded him of when he was a boy in Georgia. Only this was summer hay in Elkhart. Hay that had been reaped during the drought.

He closed his eyes, but suddenly he was not sleepy. The gunfight had him keyed up. Why had he shot the kid's hand? He should have shot him in the chest.

He looked up into the darkness, wondering where he would go next when he left Elkhart.

Maybe he should head north, into one of the mountain territories. It would be a long ride, but maybe the trail north would take him out of drought country.

The smith called from below. "I'm going to bed. There won't be any light except for the fire."

Slocum grunted in reply.

The smith was a good man. How had he survived in this godforsaken place? Maybe he was just one of those people who could stay out of trouble, wherever he was.

Slocum closed his eyes again. He tossed and turned in the hay.

The air was too hot and close under the barn roof.

He took another drink but that didn't help. He started to lie back again, but the creaking of a hinge froze him in a sitting position. Slocum reached for his gun.

Somebody had come into the stable. And Slocum was pretty sure the intruder had come for him.

3

Slocum's heart began to pound. He gripped the Colt tightly in his gun hand. The intruder kept moving below.

He should have ridden out of town when he had the chance.

How many of them had come for him? He could only hear one person moving.

Maybe the smith would hear the intruder and come out to run him off.

Slocum slowly got to his feet.

He heard scuffling along the dirt floor.

Some of the horses snorted. The intruder stopped for a moment and then began moving again. There was scuffling under the ladder.

Slocum tried to swallow but the whiskey had left his mouth dry.

The intruder began to climb the ladder. Slocum could hear the rungs creaking. A hand came over the edge of the loft.

When Slocum saw the intruder's head, he thumbed back the hammer of the Colt. "That's far enough."

The silence only lasted a moment.

A woman laughed. "Why, John. Is it always your custom to pull a gun on a girl when she comes to call?"

Slocum lowered the weapon. "You!"

Belle climbed over the edge of the loft. He could smell her perfume. She stood up to face him.

"No need for that, sir."

Slocum scowled at her. "What do you want?"

"What makes you think I want anything?"

"You're here, aren't you?"

Belle invoked the laugh again. She was good at it. Slocum wondered if she might be part of some trap.

"I only came to see if you were all right," Belle replied. "In all that commotion, I wasn't sure if you had been shot."

"I wasn't."

She moved a little closer. "You did the right thing by shooting that kid. But he'll try for revenge, John."

"He won't get the chance," Slocum replied. "I'm riding out of here first thing in the morning."

"Then we have the night," Belle said.

Slocum looked at her. "We? What about the gambler?"

Belle waved him away, giggling. "He's a fool. No, it's you I wanted to see, John."

Slocum gave a derisive chortle. "Me? I'm no slick dresser, nor am I handsome or pretty."

She sidled next to him, touching his arm. "No, but a woman doesn't always want a man who's pretty."

Slocum's heart started to pound again. He could sense her need. She wanted to lie with him. His whole body felt it.

"It got me hot in there," she said. "I love to watch men shoot it out. You were great, John. You shot that kid." She pressed her lips to his.

Slocum kept one eye over her shoulder, watching for the trap. But it never came. Belle had really come to lie with him.

His hands cupped her heaving breasts.

Belle reached down to touch his crotch. She moaned when she felt the hardness there. She fumbled with the buttons of his fly.

Slocum ran his hands down her backside. He grabbed her full bottom and squeezed her buttocks. She pressed her crotch into his.

"Lie down," she told him.

Slocum lay back on the hay.

Belle straddled him. She lifted her dress. He could see the dark patch between her thighs.

Belle lowered herself into the hay. Her soft hand closed around his member. She guided him to the wet entrance between her legs. When he penetrated her, a low moan escaped from her throat. She began to work her hips.

Slocum got tired of being on the bottom. He grabbed her ass. With one flip, he had her on her back.

"Yes," she said. "Give it to me. Let me have it with that big pistol of yours. Shoot inside me."

Slocum fell between her legs. Belle quickly guided him inside. The loft shook as he started to ride her.

"John?"

Slocum froze with his cock buried in her.

The smithy's voice rose again from below. "I heard a commotion, John. I wondered if everything was all right."

"Yeah," Slocum replied. "Go back to bed."

Belle giggled. "We're just having some fun, Ray. You go on back to bed and have sweet dreams."

"Yes, ma'am, Miss Belle."

She smiled at Slocum. "He'll probably go whip his whanger now."

"You know all the men in this town?" he asked.

"Would it matter if I did?"

"No."

He started to move again.

Belle cried her ecstasy to the night air.

Sweat poured from their bodies.

Slocum kept driving her until he felt his sap rising.

His body collapsed on top of her.

Belle hugged his shoulders. "Keep it in there till it goes soft," she told him. "Don't pull out." She kissed him.

Slocum had to roll off her. His head was spinning. He needed another shot of red-eye. He started to look for the bottle.

"What is it?" Belle asked.

"Whiskey. I had some here."

"I'll find it for you," she offered.

It took her a few minutes to locate the bottle in the dark.

Slocum did not see her pour the clear liquid into the bottle of hooch.

"Here you go," Belle said.

Slocum drank deep from the bottle.

Belle put her head on his chest. "Don't get too drunk."

Her fingers rolled his limp cock around.

Slocum felt the stiffening. She wanted it again. And he was ready to give it to her.

Belle made a whimpering noise. "Do it to me hard," she said. "And push it deep when you shoot."

"You aren't afraid of being with child?"

"No," she replied. "If I get pregnant, I can get Tyler to marry me. I think he would."

"You want to marry him?" Slocum asked. "The gambler?"

"Yeah. His family back East has some money. If we get married and go back there, they'll take care of us."

"I thought he was a gambler."

"No, that's just because he needs money. He isn't very good, but he can fleece the cowboys. He has to deal it straight, though, when he plays with Mr. Cooper."

Slocum didn't want to hear about Cooper. He wanted to top the woman again.

Falling between her legs, he prodded her wet opening. She guided him the rest of the way in. Slocum humped her hard. He humped her for all the times he was lonely on the trail. He humped her for all the lonely times to come.

Belle shook with each thrust. She kept urging him to do it harder. Slocum tried his best.

He felt his release coming again. His body went limp. He buried his cock to the hilt. His discharge erupted inside her.

Belle cried out.

Slocum collapsed with his face in her breasts.

Belle stroked his head. "Go to sleep, Johnny boy. Go sound asleep."

Slocum closed his eyes. He didn't even feel it when Belle rolled him off her. His back hit the hay. He was asleep in a few seconds. The potion that she had given him had taken effect.

The door downstairs creaked again. "Belle?"

"Up here, Tyler."

Belle was pulling down her skirt as Jensen ascended the ladder.

The gambler gaped at her. "You did it with him."

"Oh, shut up and check his pockets."

"Where's the liveryman?" Jensen asked.

Belle shrugged. "Downstairs beating his meat."

Jensen slapped her.

Belle didn't even flinch. "Okay, you hit me. Now go through his pockets before I kill you."

Jensen rolled Slocum. He counted the wad of money. Belle watched over his shoulder.

"Is it enough?" she asked.

Jensen nodded. "Yep. All we have to do is get to Oklahoma City."

"The stage leaves at dawn," Belle replied. "Is it here yet?"

"No, but it should be soon."

They both looked down at Slocum.

"He was a fool," Jensen said.

Belle sighed. "I suppose."

Jensen slipped the money into his coat pocket. "We have to pack."

"Wait until the saloon is empty," she replied. "We don't want to attract any attention."

"What if somebody sees us getting on the stage?" Jensen asked.

"We'll say that we're going to visit my sick aunt in Oklahoma City. We'll be back in two weeks."

Jensen nodded and started for the ladder. "At least we'll be out of this town."

Belle looked at Slocum one more time. "Sorry, cowboy."

Slocum only snored in reply.

Slocum opened his eyes. His head began to spin. The heat seemed unbearable around him. He tried to sit up but the pain was too much. He groaned.

"John?"

The voice came from below the loft.

Thornton climbed the ladder and stuck his head over the top rung. "You okay, John?"

Slocum moaned again. "Water."

"Sure."

Thornton went down the ladder. In a few minutes he came back with a bucket and dipper. He set the bucket next to Slocum.

Slocum drank from the dipper. His stomach turned over. He gagged on the water.

"Throw it on me," he said.

Thornton frowned. "What?"

"Throw the bucket of water on me."

"Okay, if that's what you want."

Slocum cried out when the water hit him. But it revived him. He sat up in the loft.

"Where's Belle?" Thornton asked.

"Belle!"

The woman had been there. They had rolled in the hay. Slocum knew what he had to do next, but he didn't want to do it in front of the blacksmith.

"Thanks for the water," he told Thornton.

"I was wondering," the smithy said. "Do you want to sell me that sorrel? I'll give you top dollar."

"We'll talk about it later," Slocum replied. "Give me time to get my head back."

Thornton frowned, but he went down the ladder.

Slocum immediately checked the pockets of his pants. All of his money was gone. The woman had taken it.

He couldn't remember very much of it. He had been drunk. He had passed out on top of her. It was all a blurry dream.

Slocum leaned back on the straw. At least he had paid the livery in advance. Maybe he should sell the sorrel, get a mount for a little less money. If he turned a profit on the gelding, he wouldn't have to stay in Elkhart to find work.

Then he remembered the shooting. Slocum wondered if the kid knew where he was staying.

It would probably be smarter if he just rode on. No matter that he was broke. He could always shovel shit somewhere down the line and make a few dollars to help him along. There was no need to stay in Elkhart, not after all the trouble.

He tried to stand up again. His body ached. His head spun. The woman had put something in his whiskey; then she had cleaned him out. Maybe he could find her and get his money back.

Voices rose suddenly in the hot air. It had to be past noon. The stable was steamy inside.

Slocum heard the stableman talking to someone down in the barn. Slocum reached for his Colt. Somebody started up the ladder.

"John," the liveryman called, "it's the sheriff. He wants to talk to you, John. He's coming up."

Slocum eased the Colt back into his holster.

He saw the badge as it came over the ladder. A husky man with a ruddy face topped by a wide-brimmed Stetson glared at him.

"You the one they call John?" the sheriff asked.

Slocum nodded.

"I'm Sheriff Herman Peters. I have to ask you for your gun."

Slocum's eyes narrowed. "Are you arresting me?"

Peters drew his gun, a big Colt Peacemaker. "Come on, John."

"Now wait, Sheriff."

Peters waved the barrel of the Colt. "Drop your weapon. Reach for it with your left hand."

Slocum had to do it. The sheriff had the drop on him. And there was no place to run, unless he wanted to dive two stories to the ground below. He dropped the Colt .36 into the straw.

"Now move away from it," the sheriff said.

Slocum started for the loft window, thinking that the fall might be better than going to jail.

"The other way," the sheriff said. "Toward the wall."

Slocum figured the old boy was pretty sharp. He put his back to the wall. Peters kept watching him as he picked up the .36.

"Don't get no ideas about running," Peters said. "I got men outside with rifles. Joe!"

The deputy called from the bottom of the ladder. "Right here, Sheriff!"

Peters waved the Colt. "You first."

Slocum climbed down the ladder. Another man was waiting for him. He tied Slocum's hands behind his back. The deputy pushed him toward the street. "Let's go."

There were more men outside. A lot of deputies for such a small town, Slocum thought. Slocum wondered if the man named Cooper was paying all of their salaries, too.

The jailhouse was small and hot. Slocum's cell had a stool and a slop bucket. Slocum hated the sound of the door slamming shut. And it was even worse when the key turned, locking him behind the iron bars.

4

Slocum had been locked up many times in his life. The jail was always in some godforsaken place, and the Elkhart jail was no exception. Three dirty walls and a row of iron bars. Bugs scampered in and out of the cracks in the floor.

He leaned back on the sagging mattress of the cot. Corn shucks rustled under his body. He wondered if this would be the last time. Would they hang him for shooting the kid?

If the sheriff was on the payroll of the local ranchers, he would do whatever they told him. They might tell him to hang Slocum, to get rid of the drifter who had caused so much trouble in the saloon.

He tried to sleep, but it was too hot. Sweat poured off him. His mouth was dry from the whiskey he had drunk the night before.

Slocum cursed the woman for stealing his money. Even if there was a fine or bail to post, he would not be able to pay. He might have to sit in jail for a couple of weeks or months.

What the hell had he done, anyway? Gunfights were an everyday occurrence west of the Mississippi.

Slocum had gotten involved in the wrong fight. He never should have drawn on the kid. It hadn't been his business. He had acted too impulsively.

The door to the jailhouse swung open. Sheriff Peters strode in with a tray in his hands. "You ready to eat, drifter?"

Slocum sighed. At least they wanted to feed him—maybe to fatten him up for the hangman.

Peters slipped the tray under the iron door. "Not much, just some stew and corn bread."

Slocum ate quickly. The food was salty and he asked for water. Peters gave him a jug.

"Got us a drought hereabouts," Peters said. "Been causin' a passel of trouble."

Slocum nodded. "So I heard."

Peters wiped sweat from his forehead. "Damned heat. Look here, boy, you got a name?"

"John."

"John what?"

"John Smith," Slocum lied.

The sheriff chortled. "Somehow I knew that was gonna be it. John Smith. That ain't your real name."

Slocum just kept quiet. He figured the sheriff did not have any posters on him. He hadn't done anything wrong in Oklahoma, not in this part of the country, anyway.

Peters shook his head. "Well, John Smith, you know why I locked you up? Huh?"

"I shot that kid," Slocum replied.

The sheriff laughed. "No, that ain't it. Hell, you woulda done me a favor to kill him. I'd do it myself if—"

He hesitated.

Slocum finished the sentence for him. "If Cooper hadn't told you to leave him alone."

Peters's eyes narrowed. "What you know about Cooper? You working for him?"

"No. The woman told me."

"Belle?"

Slocum nodded. "She told me just before she cleaned me out. Got me drunk and took every red cent I own."

Peters grinned. "Yeah?"

"I'd like to try to get it back," Slocum said. "That way I could pay any fine you might—"

"You're shit out of luck, Smith. The woman and that dandy gambler took off on the stage first thing this mornin'. Said they was goin' to Oklahoma City to visit her sick aunt."

Slocum shook his head. "Damn!"

Peters glared at him again. "Okay, boy, why don't you tell me why you really came to Elkhart. You a hired gun?"

"No."

"They say you shot pretty good in the saloon. Said you drew quick and let the kid have it in the hand."

Slocum slid the empty tray under the cell door. "I never should have gotten involved."

The sheriff exhaled. "No, but you did. And there's people in these parts ain't gonna take kindly to that."

Slocum drank from the water jug. The liquid tasted like metal, but it eased the dryness in his throat.

"Come on," Peters said, "tell me why you came here, Smith. You ain't no cowpuncher."

"I'm just drifting through, Sheriff. You let me out of this cell, I'll be on my way. I'll put Elkhart behind me and you'll never see me again."

"It ain't that easy," Peters replied. "But you tell me who hired you, and maybe we can work somethin' out."

Slocum leaned back on the cot. "I've said all I have to say, Sheriff. If you don't believe me, then there's nothing else I can do."

Peters wiped more sweat from his face. "That ain't what I wanted to hear, Smith."

Slocum just kept quiet.

"See," the sheriff went on, "I got to hold you. Oh, I know it was just a gunfight. But you did shoot a man in my town. That's happened before, but this was a man who works for Mr. Cooper."

Slocum realized that the sheriff was going to use him as a scapegoat. All he had done was wing the kid with one shot.

"Main reason I locked you up was to save your life," the sheriff continued. "Mr. Cooper hears about this, he might send somebody else to look for you. Not that the kid has any friends. Even the men who work with him ain't very loyal. You get my drift?"

"Let me go," Slocum said. "I'll be out of town in two minutes."

"I wish it was that easy," Peters replied. "You seem like a rough sort, but you don't seem that bad."

Slocum looked up at the ceiling of the jailhouse. He knew he had done wrong in his time. Maybe it was all catching up to him now.

"It's like this," Peters went on, "I've got to hold you. There's a law about firin' a gun in town. Now, I can't hang you for it. Not that I'd want to, but there's time to serve if you can't pay the fine."

Slocum grimaced. If the woman hadn't cleaned him out, he would be able to pay the fine. Now he would have to sweat it out in the Elkhart jail.

"How much is the fine?" he asked.

The sheriff shrugged. "Does it matter?"

"You got my gun," Slocum said. "And I got a horse that the liveryman wants to buy."

"I'll look into it," the sheriff replied.

"Sure you will."

"Don't get smart with me, Smith. I can keep you in here as long as I want. It's my jail."

"I wouldn't bet on that, Sheriff!" The voice had come from behind the lawman.

Slocum looked up. A woman and a man stood in the doorway of the jailhouse. Slocum recognized the woman as the daughter of the rifleman who had been shot by the kid.

Peters turned to frown at them. "Miss Wheeler, this ain't none of your affair."

The pretty blond girl started to move into the jailhouse.

A deputy tried to stop her. "She wouldn't listen to me, Sheriff."

The girl glared at Peters. "Sheriff, this is Tom Stewart. He's a lawyer from Oklahoma City. He's come here to start a new practice and I've hired him to help me get this man out of jail."

Slocum stood holding onto the bars, staring out at the woman.

Peters sighed. "Let her through."

"What about the lawboy?" the deputy asked.

"Him, too."

Slocum watched the woman and the lawyer as they came through the doorway.

"Sheriff, I'd like to know the charges against this man," the lawyer said.

"Firin' a gun in the town limits," Peters replied.

"Have you assessed a fine against him?" the lawyer asked.

Peters nodded. "Fifty dollars or fifty days in jail."

Slocum winced. Fifty days. Almost two months.

Miss Wheeler reached into her purse. "Here, fifty dollars."

Peters groaned. "Aw, Miss Wheeler, you don't want to get involved with this drifter."

"He stood up for my father," the girl said. "I owe him a chance to get out of this place."

The lawyer nodded. "The fine has been paid, Sheriff. You can't hold him any longer."

"Amen," Slocum said.

Peters was not sure what to do next. He had guns, but the woman had the law on her side.

"I'm waiting, Sheriff," the girl said.

Peters reluctantly turned the key in the lock. "Okay, Smith. You're free."

Slocum stepped out of the cell. The hot air suddenly seemed fresh. He had to get to the stable and get his horse.

The girl looked at him with pretty blue eyes. "Sir, my name is Rebecca Wheeler. I want to thank you for saving my father's life."

Slocum nodded. "We're square. Sheriff, I want my gun."

Peters gave Slocum his holster and the Colt .36. "Don't hang around, Smith."

"Don't worry, Sheriff. I won't."

Slocum strode out of the jailhouse past the two guards.

The woman and the lawyer followed him.

"Mr. Smith," Rebecca Wheeler called, "you owe me fifty dollars."

Slocum kept walking toward the stable. "I thought you paid my fine because I saved your daddy's life."

"I couldn't afford to pay that," Rebecca replied. "But I did. And you still owe me."

Slocum did not reply.

Tom Stewart had to offer his opinion. "Mr. Smith, Miss Wheeler has spent her last dollar to free you from—"

"Save it," Slocum said. "I didn't ask her to bail me out. But since she did, I'm getting the hell out of here."

"Your language!" Stewart said.

"I've heard it before," Rebecca told him.

They followed Slocum to the front of the stable.

Rebecca Wheeler was not ready to give up. "Mr. Smith—if that is your name—I need help at my ranch. With my father in bed with that wound, I need someone to help run the cattle."

"I sure hope you find somebody," Slocum replied.

The stableman looked up when he saw Slocum enter. "Howdy, John. You come for that sorrel?"

"I need it now," Slocum replied.

Thornton grimaced. "Ah, you caught me, John. Somethin' happened last night that you prob'ly won't like."

Slocum sighed. Just what he needed. More bad news.

Thornton noticed the woman. "Good day, Miss Wheeler. And I don't believe I know this gentleman."

"Stewart. Tom Stewart. If you should ever need legal counsel, I'm opening an office behind the general store. Mind you, it's only territorial law, but I—"

"Sure," Thornton said. "You're lookin' mighty pretty, Miss Wheeler."

Rebecca ignored the compliment. "Mr. Smith—"

Slocum turned to the liveryman. "You had bad news for me?"

"Your horse was stolen in the night," Thornton replied. "They left your gear, but the sorrel just disappeared."

Slocum gritted his teeth. "Damn!"

"I know what you mean," Thornton replied. "I could have gotten a hundred dollars for that mount."

Rebecca threw out her hands. "There you are, Mr. Smith. You're stranded and in debt to me."

"I'm busted," Slocum replied.

Stewart looked at the tall drifter. "Yes, but you're still under legal obligation to Miss Wheeler. Moral obligation as well."

"You don't have a horse, either," Rebecca added.

Slocum bristled. He knew the girl was right. There was no way to square the debt with her unless he went to work for her.

Rebecca was not ready to give up on him. "Mr. Smith, if you're going to—"

Slocum raised his hand. "Might as well call me John. Go on, say your whole piece now."

"I'm sure you can reach an arrangement," the lawyer chimed in.

"All right, John. I have a wagon outside. Mr. Stewart is going to accompany me to my ranch. If you would come along, I can let you work the fifty dollars off. A dollar a day is usually what I pay my hands, but if you'll come to work for me, I'll double that."

Slocum sighed defeatedly. He needed work. The cards had fallen that way. He had to play the hand that he had been dealt.

"I'm really sorry," Thornton said. "I'm puttin' on a new latch."

Slocum started out of the livery. "Little late for that."

Rebecca and Stewart followed him.

Thornton came after him carrying his saddle and saddle-bags. "Mr. Smith, you don't want to forget your gear."

The buckboard wagon waited across the street.

"Are you coming with me?" Rebecca asked.

Slocum nodded. "For now."

He could always run out later, after it was dark.

They boarded the wagon. Thornton threw Slocum's gear in the back. Stewart also sat in the rear of the wagon.

Rebecca picked up the reins. "You won't regret this, Mr. Smith."

"Yes I will."

She started to shake the reins.

Somebody moved in front of the wagon.

Slocum looked down at the kid he had shot the night before. The kid wore a bandage around his wounded hand. He glared up at Slocum with vengeful eyes. Slocum's hand dropped beside his Colt.

"You're gonna pay for this," the kid said, holding up his injured paw. "You better thank your maker that I can't shoot with my other hand."

"Get out of the way," Rebecca said.

The kid smiled. "Well, Miss Becky, don't you look nigh on good enough to eat."

Rebecca Wheeler shook the reins.

The buckboard lurched forward, knocking the kid out of the way.

"You hear me?" the kid cried. "You're gonna pay."

Slocum figured he had already paid plenty.

The buckboard rolled out of Elkhart.

Rebecca shook her head. "That damned Cimarron Kid!"

Slocum just sat there, trying to figure a way to get out of Oklahoma.

5

Dust swirled around the buckboard. Slocum sat next to the woman, keeping silent. He did not want to like her, but it was hard not to feel his heart softening. She was pretty and brave, two things that were almost irresistible in a woman.

Slocum could see signs of the drought everywhere he looked. There were withered plants and trees all around him. Cornfields that should have been green sat dead and brown alongside the road.

"We've barely been able to keep our cattle fed," Rebecca commented. "We can't drive them to market, either."

Slocum did not reply.

"Have you worked cattle before, Mr. Smith?"

Slocum nodded. "Some."

They rolled toward a distant fence. Slocum saw the name of the ranch as they got closer. The sign read: Lazy River C, Robert Wheeler, Owner. The buckboard went past the sign.

"We call it the Lazy River C because the Cimarron River runs through our property," Rebecca said. "It hasn't dried up completely, so we've been able to water our cows. The ones that have died starved to death."

Slocum made no comment. He figured it wouldn't matter much longer. He was going to leave the first chance he got. He'd head north, where the water flowed through the Rockies, or maybe he would go east, to Oklahoma City. He could look for the gambler and the woman, and get some of his money back—if he could find them.

The wagon approached several dusty structures. A large house sat next to a long bunkhouse. A group of men had gathered in front of the bunkhouse. Rebecca guided the wagon toward them.

The men watched them approach.

Rebecca reined the horse and regarded them with a frown. "Why aren't you men on the range, tending the herd?"

A red-haired man stepped forward. "Miss Wheeler, we heard you're out of money. Is that true?"

Rebecca lowered her eyes. "You've heard correctly, Mr. Henderson."

The men spoke among themselves for a moment.

Henderson shook his head. "That ain't good, Miss Wheeler. I been with your paw a long time. I ain't gonna leave him in the lurch, but some of these other hands don't feel the same way."

"That's right," one of the men said. "If you can't pay me, then I can't work for you, Miss Wheeler."

"You'll all get your money when we take the cattle to market," Rebecca insisted. "I won't cheat you."

They muttered to each other.

Slocum had seen it before. Men wouldn't hang on if there was no chance of pay. Loyalty went out the window when the dollar a day disappeared. She had promised Slocum two dollars a day. That was money through her fingers now.

Henderson exhaled. "Miss Wheeler, you know as well as I do that we can't drive those cows to market. There ain't no water between here and Kansas. Once we leave the Cimarron, we'd never get those cows to Abilene, even if it is a short drive."

Rebecca flushed. "Very well, Mr. Henderson. How many of you want to leave? Let's see your hands."

Out of the twelve men, nine raised their hands.

"How much do I owe you?"

"They each got five dollars apiece coming to them," Henderson said.

She took out a pouch with the last of her life savings. She had probably figured that the men were going to quit. She really did need Slocum on board.

Rebecca threw the money in the dust. "There. You can all go to work for Cooper now. I hope I never see any of your faces again."

Henderson tipped back his hat. "I'm stayin' on, Miss Rebecca. Me and these other two. We figger we've been with your daddy too long to leave now. As long as you feed us, we'll be here."

"Thank you, Mr. Henderson. As long as we have beef on this ranch, you'll have plenty to eat."

Henderson looked at Slocum. "New hand?"

"Yes," Rebecca replied. "Mr. John Smith. There's plenty of room in the bunkhouse now."

Slocum climbed down. He got his gear from the back. He had decided to really work off the fifty dollars. He wanted to square his debt with the girl.

Rebecca turned the buckboard toward the large house. Dust swirled in her tracks. Slocum noticed that she was crying as she turned away.

Henderson shook his head. "She's a good woman. Come all the way back here from some fancy school in the East just to help her paw."

Slocum nodded. "Show me where to put my gear."

Henderson started for the bunkhouse. He was older, some gray hair among the red strands. His hands and face had been worn by hard work.

Some of the others laughed at him.

"Gonna stay on, Henderson?"

"You're a fool."

"Ride with us."

"Yeah, Cooper is hirin'."

Henderson glanced back at them. "You boys go on. There's more to this than a few dollars. If you sign on with Cooper, then you deserve whatever happens to you. Now, git."

He turned toward the door.

Slocum followed him into the bunkhouse. He figured Henderson to be a good man. His loyalties seemed to lie with the Wheeler family.

"Put your gear there," he said. "You can take your pick of the bunks. You got a mount?"

Slocum shook his head.

"We'll get you one in the mornin'," Henderson replied. "Not much to choose from. We been runnin' low on oats."

Slocum dropped his gear against the wall. Shadows were growing longer over the ranch. It would be dark soon.

"How'd you meet Miss Rebecca?" Henderson asked.

Slocum shrugged. "Ran into her in Elkhart."

"You the one who shot the Cimarron Kid?"

Slocum frowned at him. "You heard about that?"

"Don't take word long to get around," Henderson replied. "They say you saved Mr. Wheeler's life."

"Maybe I did."

Henderson smiled. "I'm proud to meet the man who shot the kid. He's been causin' trouble since Cooper hired him."

Slocum sat down on a bunk. "That so?"

"Yeah. There's gonna be more trouble, too. What with—"

Slocum raised a hand. "I don't want to hear it, Henderson. I'm here to work off a debt. Miss Wheeler bailed me out of that hellhole jail. As soon as I'm square with her, I'm riding out."

Henderson's eyes narrowed. "You a hard case?"

"As hard as they come."

Two other men came into the bunkhouse. They were the ones who had sworn allegiance to the Wheeler family. Their eyes fell on Slocum.

"This here is Bick and Freeman," Henderson said. "They been with Wheeler almost as long as I have."

Slocum did not look up.

Bick was a short, balding man. Freeman was skinny with a pointed face. They both sat on bunks.

"He's the one who shot the kid," Henderson said.

"That right?" Bick asked.

Slocum sighed. "I shot him."

"Hey," Freeman said, "you sound like a rebel. Where you hail from, partner?"

Slocum sat up. "Georgia. Anything wrong with that?"

"Nosiree," Freeman replied. "Fought for the gray myself. Glad to meet a fellow rebel."

Slocum leaned back on the bed.

Henderson looked at his men. "Well, I guess this is what you'd call a skeleton crew. Somebody's got to ride night herd."

Freeman nodded. "I'll do it. Them cows ain't goin' far from the river, even if it is down to a trickle."

"I better start makin' a pot of stew," Bick said. "Won't be much to it but meat and water."

Slocum closed his eyes. He heard the others riding away. It was a long time after dark before he heard more horses approaching the ranch.

Henderson gazed out a window. "Damn. I hope there's no more trouble."

Slocum reached for his Colt, making sure it was ready.

Then he sat up and looked out the window.

"It's Cooper," Henderson informed him.

They watched three riders dismount and walk up to the door of the ranch house. When they knocked, Rebecca came to the door. She seemed reluctant to let them in, but the lawyer was there beside her and he admitted the riders to the house.

Slocum stood on the porch of the bunkhouse next to Henderson and Bick. He wondered if he would see gunplay on his first night at the ranch. His hand rested on the butt of his Colt.

Henderson looked at him. "I need to know, Smith. Are you a hired gun like ever'body's sayin'?"

Slocum stared at the house. "I can take care of myself. But I'm not a hired gun."

"How'd you stand up to the kid?" Henderson asked.

"I just did."

Bick held a rifle ready, in case trouble started.

"I wonder if we should go up there," Henderson said.

They heard the voices rising in the dry night air. Somebody was arguing inside the house.

Slocum touched the butt of the Colt. Maybe the woman had hired him for his gun. The sheriff had thought Slocum was a gunslinger. And there seemed to be plenty of trouble around.

"Cooper didn't come to shoot it out," Henderson said. "Leastways not this time."

"What you think he's up to?" Bick asked.

"Same thing as before," Henderson replied. "He wants to buy her out. But she's not gonna sell. Not that girl."

The heated words continued inside the ranch house.

Slocum turned to Henderson. "Why does Cooper want to buy her out?"

He figured it was better to know what was going on.

Henderson sighed. "Water. Plain and simple. The Cimarron is the closest water in the territory. River runs right through the Lazy River C. That's how the place got its name."

"Cooper wants to water his cows," Bick said.

"And she won't let him?" Slocum asked.

Henderson shook his head. "She's not going to turn Cooper away, Smith. Won't turn anybody away. She could do it, by law. But she won't. She ain't that kind."

Slocum frowned. "Then what's the trouble?"

"All of Cooper's water has dried up," Henderson replied. "He had creeks and ponds, but they're all gone. He's afraid now. He wants the Lazy River C for his own. He figgers the girl might change her mind."

"Yeah," Bick said. "Some men ain't happy enough to share. They got to have it all for theirselves."

Slocum had seen it before. Greed could twist a man around. Rebecca Wheeler was trying to do the right thing, but Cooper wasn't going to let her do it. Some men just had to make trouble.

"She's lucky that there's no debt on the ranch," Henderson said. "Her daddy was smart enough to pay off the bank a couple of years ago, when things were flush. If there was a note, Cooper'd probably try to buy it."

"He knows she's broke," Bick added. "He's bought out ever'body that went bust. But he still don't have enough water."

"Water," Henderson said. "Funny how somethin' like that could drive a man to do wrong."

"What's he done?" Slocum asked.

"You saw it," Henderson replied. "He offered day wages to Wheeler's crew. And he sent the kid around to bother Miss Rebecca. He knew that Wheeler would try to defend his daughter's good name. Thought the kid would kill him. But you put a stop to that, Smith."

Slocum chortled. "My good luck."

"Look!" Bick said. "They're coming out."

Slocum watched as the three riders emerged from the ranch house. "Which one is Cooper?"

"The fat shit," Henderson replied. "Lord, that Yankee ain't made nothin' but trouble since he came here."

"Yankee?" Slocum said.

Henderson nodded. "Rode with Sherman, or so I heard. He was an officer. One of those bastards who cut a path through Georgia."

Slocum looked at him. "You ain't just tellin' me that so I'll stay on, are you?"

"I ain't one to lie," Henderson replied.

"Yankee," Slocum said again.

The lawyer was at the door of the ranch house. He argued with the riders for a moment. Then he closed the door.

The riders mounted up. One of them rode toward the bunkhouse. He reined up in front of Slocum and the others.

"You men want to come work for Cooper?"

Henderson spat at the ground. "Ain't workin' for no Yankee sidewinder. Now git outta here."

The rider laughed. "Well, you'll be workin' for him sooner or later. This place is goin' under."

Slocum glared at the rider. "You heard him. Clear on out."

The man peered at the lanky son of Dixie. "You rebels are all alike. You talk big, but you ain't got what it takes."

"Ask the kid if I got what it takes," Slocum replied.

"Yeah?" the rider said. "So you're the one who winged Cimarron. Mr. Cooper is paying top dollar for gunhands."

"He's gonna be payin' for your funeral if you don't get the hell out of here," Slocum said.

The rider hesitated. "Hey, boys, if you—"

"That goes double for me," Henderson said. "Git."

"You can't make it, Henderson. Not even with this rebel gun. We got you outnumbered ten to one."

"Maybe," Henderson replied. "But right now we got you outnumbered three to one. Now get on over there with that Yankee boss of yours."

The rider trotted away, stirring dust in the night.

Slocum turned away and walked back into the bunkhouse. The others came in behind him.

"Cooper does have us out-gunned," Bick said.

Henderson shot him a dirty look. "Free country, Bick. If Miss Rebecca doesn't want to sell out to that bastard, then I'm with her. How about you, Smith?"

Slocum leaned back on his bunk. He did not reply. He owed the woman fifty dollars. At two dollars a day, his debt would be paid in twenty-five days. If the trouble came in that time, Slocum knew he would have to be a part of it.

6

The rooster woke Slocum from a dreamless sleep. He sat up on the bunk. For a moment, he had forgotten where he was. Then he remembered: the Lazy River C.

The woman had gotten him out of jail because he had saved her father. But now he owed her.

Slocum gazed across the shadowed bunkhouse.

Henderson stood in the predawn darkness. "You want a cup of coffee?" he asked Slocum.

The tall man from Georgia nodded.

Henderson filled a tin cup with steaming brown liquid. "It'll take the shine off your teeth, but it's better than nothin'."

Slocum sipped the bitter coffee. He put down the cup and rolled a cigarette then lit it from the fire in the wood stove.

"Wouldn't have another one of those, would you?" Henderson asked.

Slocum tossed him the pouch.

Henderson rolled a cigarette. After he lit it, he handed the pouch back to Slocum. They smoked as they watched the sun grow brighter through the window.

"Freeman ain't back yet," Henderson said.

Slocum did not say anything.

"I got a feelin'," Henderson went on. "Cooper's gonna make a move. He tried to get the kid to do his dirty work, but it didn't work out. You were the knot in the rope, Smith."

"Call me John."

Henderson looked at him. "I'm figgerin' that neither one of them is your real name. You look like a man who forgot your real name a long time ago. But it don't matter. We got to start stayin' with the herd in case of trouble."

Slocum nodded toward the window. "This looks like Freeman."

Dust rose in the still, morning air. Freeman came galloping toward the bunkhouse. He dismounted, entered the bunkhouse, and walked up to Henderson. "Two more dead steers," he said.

Henderson sighed. "I reckon we're lucky it ain't more. Bick! Come on, we got to ride. Freeman, you get your sleep. But then come on out. We're stayin' with the herd."

Slocum finished his coffee while Bick rolled out of his bunk, grumbling.

Slocum figured there wasn't going to be any breakfast. Then Henderson pulled a pan of corn bread out of the stove's oven. It steamed in the warm air. The smell made Slocum hungry.

"We got some molasses," Henderson told him. "No butter though. The milk cows didn't make it in this heat."

Slocum ate the corn bread and molasses.

When Henderson had finished, he looked at Bick. "Run up to the stable and get John a horse."

Bick left the bunkhouse, and Slocum said, "I could have gotten my own horse."

Henderson shook his head. "Bick knows our remuda better'n any of us. He'll get you a good mount."

Slocum went out onto the front porch of the bunkhouse. He gazed over the spread. Dust seemed to hang in the air, unstirred by the slight trace of a breeze. It looked like a fire had leveled the plain.

Bick came back with a stout dapple-gray.

Slocum went inside to get his gear.

"We've taken pretty good care of the horses," Henderson said. "I wish I could say the same for the cows."

Slocum went out to saddle the gray. It was a gelding. It took the saddle without any trouble.

Slocum started to mount up.

A voice from behind stopped him. "Mr. Smith!"

He turned to see Rebecca Wheeler walking toward the bunkhouse. She was wearing a calico dress. Her blond hair was tied up behind her head. Even on a hot, dusty morning, she looked fresh and beautiful.

"Mr. Smith, my father would like to see you."

Slocum gestured back to Henderson, who had come out onto the porch. "I got to work, Miss Wheeler. I don't think Henderson can spare me."

"Go on," Henderson said. "You can catch up."

"Yes," Rebecca said, "it won't take long."

Slocum nodded. He tied the reins of the gelding to the porch of the bunkhouse. Rebecca led him toward the ranch house. "He wants to thank you for saving his life," she said.

Slocum figured he could not blame a man for being grateful. It was polite, the gesture of a true gentleman. Slocum had once considered himself a true gentleman, though the feeling had long since disappeared.

He followed the woman into the house. It was dusty inside, but the place had a fine air to it. Rebecca apologized for the dust, saying that it was hard to keep the house clean in the drought.

She led Slocum to the door of a bedroom. Her father was sitting propped up in bed. His shoulder was bandaged.

"I've brought Mr. Smith, Father."

Wheeler looked up. "I understand you're the one who winged the Cimarron Kid."

Slocum nodded. "Yes, sir."

"I'm not sir," Wheeler replied. "I'm Robert. Bob to my friends. You can call me Bob."

Slocum just stood there with his hat in hand.

"You know about our business here?" Wheeler asked.

Slocum sighed. "Yes. Henderson told me."

"Good man, Henderson." Wheeler coughed.

Rebecca got him a glass of water.

He drank and then looked at Slocum again. "You can run out if this isn't your kind of trouble."

"No," Slocum said. "I owe a debt to your daughter. She rescued me from that jail in Elkhart. I plan to work it off."

"Then what?" Wheeler asked.

Slocum shrugged. "I'll deal with that when the time comes."

Wheeler leaned back on the pillow. "I'm sure you will."

Slocum looked straight at the pale man. "Mr. Wheeler, I'm not a hired gun. I'll work, but I'm not going to kill anybody for you."

"My father doesn't want to kill anyone!" Rebecca cried. "It's Cooper who does all the killing."

Wheeler patted his daughter's hand. "Now, now, Becky. Mr. Smith here has a right to do what's best for him."

Slocum started to turn away.

"Smith!"

"Yes, sir?"

"Come in early," Wheeler said. "About noon. I have something I want you to do."

"If Henderson can spare me. I—"

"This is my ranch," Wheeler replied. "You take orders from me. I want you to be here no later than midday. Is that clear, Mr. Smith?"

"Yes, sir."

Slocum left the bedroom. He strode down the hall. Rebecca followed him to the front door.

"My father didn't mean anything, Mr. Smith. He—"

Slocum's piercing green eyes met hers. "Your daddy was right. It's his ranch. If I work for him, I do what he says."

"Thank you for understanding," Rebecca said.

Slocum replied, "I don't understand, Miss Wheeler; I take orders. And after I've worked off that fifty dollars, I don't take orders anymore. Is that clear?"

"You're a hard man, Mr. Smith."

"I'm glad you know that, Miss Wheeler. It's better that you find out now, before anyone gets hurt." Slocum strode away from her.

Rebecca bit her lip as she watched him go. She could not understand how a man's heart became like iron. She had never been taught about such things at her fancy Eastern school.

Henderson was waiting for Slocum, holding the reins of the gelding. "What's the word, John?"

"I'm only working a half day today. Mr. Wheeler's orders."

Slocum swung into the saddle.

Henderson mounted up, too.

Bick fell in beside them on a roan mare. "Half day? Man, some boys get all the breaks."

"Shut up," Henderson said. "I'm sure Mr. Wheeler has somethin' in mind for Smith."

They spurred their mounts and headed west in a cloud of dust.

Slocum had never seen such a sorry-looking herd. The steers were thin and scraggly. They stood on the banks of the Cimarron River, pushing their noses in the ribbon of water.

The cattle had eaten all of the vegetation along the banks of the river. Slocum wondered how long they would last. Dead steers were scattered along the Cimarron, attracting buzzards in the sky.

Henderson drew his rifle and fired at the circling shapes. The gunfire didn't even scare them. Some of the birds swept down on carcasses a few miles away.

"Dad-blamed vultures," Henderson said.

They had chased off a hundred of them when they rode up on the herd.

"The water's all that keeps 'em from dyin'," Henderson said, nodding toward the herd. "Some of 'em just fall over anyway."

Slocum shifted in his saddle. "Don't reckon there's much hay hereabouts."

"S'posed to have a wagonload arrivin' any day," Henderson replied. "Comin' down from Nebraska. Things ain't so bad up that way."

"Must cost plenty," Slocum said.

Henderson sighed. "It's what broke the Wheelers. But they've got to keep these cows alive. It's the only way they're gonna make it."

Slocum rode slowly around the herd. He counted five hundred head. Not a bad count, if they could somehow fatten them up and get them to market.

He reined back on the gelding. His head was already figuring things. He wanted to help save the Wheeler place. But why? It wasn't his lookout.

The girl. She had him in a way that women sometimes got a man. He didn't want to care about her, but he did.

Rebecca was a loyal woman—loyal to her father and to the ranch. Sometimes in the dusty towns and back alleys, a man forgot that such women existed.

He urged the gelding along the riverbank. The herd parted as he rode through them.

Slocum hated punching cows, but there wasn't much to handling this docile bunch of dogies. There were no strays. None of the steers wanted to leave the waters of the Cimarron.

"John!"

Slocum looked up. Henderson was pointing to the east. Slocum saw the dust swirling on the horizon. Somebody was coming.

Slocum trotted over to Henderson. The red-haired man had drawn his rifle from the scabbard. Slocum wished he had a Winchester. He had to settle for his side arm. He drew the Colt and spun the cylinder.

Bick came riding up beside them. "What is it, Mr. Henderson?"

"Trouble."

A rider came ahead of the dust cloud. When he drew nearer, Slocum saw the bandaged hand. The Cimarron Kid cantered up and slid to a stop a few feet in front of them.

The kid smiled. "Well, if it ain't the rebel. How you doin', Reb?"

Slocum held his Colt in his hand.

"We don't want no bother," Henderson said. "You hear me, Kid?"

"Hey, call me Jimmy like ever'body else," the kid replied.

Slocum kept his green eyes on the sandy-haired punk. He had switched his gun to the other side, but Slocum figured he was no threat with his gun hand in a bandage.

"I ain't callin' you nothin'," Henderson replied. "You ride back and tell your hands to go home."

"Ain't doin' it," the kid replied. "Wheeler gave us permission to water. You don't believe me, you ask him."

Henderson turned red, but he held his tongue.

The kid nodded at Slocum. "You and me, Reb. It's gonna

happen. You just wait and see." He started to turn away.

"Kid!" Henderson cried.

"Yeah, old man?"

"You water down that way, on the east fork. You hear? Don't bring your cows up this way."

"I'll take 'em anywhere I want—"

Henderson levered the rifle and aimed it straight at him. "You mix those cows with his herd, I swear I'll plug you."

The kid smiled. "You speak mighty strong for an old man who's outnumbered ten to one."

"I don't care if you get me," Henderson replied. "I'll make sure I put a bullet through your heart."

The kid turned his horse away and loped back toward Cooper's herd.

"You shoulda killed him when you had the chance," Henderson said to Slocum. "It woulda been better."

"Why didn't you kill him just now?" Slocum retorted.

Henderson sighed. "Aw, just lay off it. We're gonna have trouble enough if they bring the herd this way."

Bick looked into the distance. "I hope they don't."

They watched nervously as the cloud of dust kept coming straight for them. The kid was testing their patience. He drove the cows within sight and then turned them toward the east fork.

"Damn him to hell," Henderson said.

Slocum holstered the Colt. "I better stay with you, Henderson. Wheeler's business can wait."

"Go on," Henderson replied. "Two or three of us—it won't matter."

"I can send Freeman back here," Slocum offered.

"No. Let him sleep. Hell, we all may be sleeping before this day is over. Six feet under."

Slocum hesitated.

"Go on," Henderson urged. "Tell Mr. Wheeler that the Cooper Cattle Company is watering here. He'll want to know."

Slocum nodded and spurred the gelding. He headed east on the opposite bank of the river.

When he passed the Cooper herd, he estimated at least two thousand head. Even Cooper's cattle outnumbered the

Wheelers'. It seemed pretty hopeless. But he still had to pay the debt.

He saw the kid staring at him.

Slocum just turned away and rode hard for the Wheelers' ranch house.

7

The sun was high overhead as Slocum approached the Wheelers' place. He saw the kitchen curtain lift and then fall again. Rebecca Wheeler had been watching for him. She came out to meet him.

Slocum dismounted and tied the gray to the hitching post in front of the house. Rebecca had a dipper of water for him. Slocum drank it down. Sweat poured off his face.

"This heat is unbearable," Rebecca said.

Slocum wiped his forehead with the back of his hand. "I reckon I should see your paw now."

Rebecca started into the house. "I want to serve you some lunch first. You look famished."

Inside, Rebecca had set the table with steaming bowls of food. There were fresh turnips and greens, sweet potatoes, corn mush, and thick slabs of roast beef. She had also made a pitcher of lemonade.

"Are you hungry, Mr. Smith?"

Slocum's mouth had begun to water. "Yes, ma'am, but I don't think I should eat."

She frowned. "But I fixed all this for you."

He nodded. "I'm obliged. But it wouldn't be right. Not with Henderson and the others missing out."

"Rest your mind," Rebecca told him. "I plan to invite them to dinner. You can't eat all of this yourself. I'll keep the leftovers until they return from the herd. There's no telling how many more meals we'll have around the Lazy River C."

"That's no way to talk, Rebecca!" Robert Wheeler was

standing in the archway that led into the dining room. He looked pale and worried.

"Sit down, John," he told Slocum. "Don't let my daughter's ill humor discourage you."

Wheeler looked over his good shoulder. "Where's Mr. Stewart?"

"Still working," Rebecca replied. "I served him a plate in your study."

Wheeler sat down. "Will you join me, Mr. Smith?"

Slocum took a place at the table. He began to spoon small helpings onto his plate. He didn't want to eat more than his share. The drought had made big meals rare.

"Mr. Stewart is arranging all my affairs," Wheeler said. "I want everything in order in the event that something should happen to me."

Slocum looked sideways at him. "You gonna sell out to that Yankee?"

"I'm not sure," Wheeler replied. "But let's have our meal. We can talk later."

Slocum tried to use good manners in front of the woman. She kept smiling at him. She didn't seem the type to go for a rough drifter, but a man could never really be sure what was in a woman's heart.

When they had finished eating, Wheeler asked his daughter to get a bottle of bourbon from his liquor cabinet and also to bring his box of cigars. He offered Slocum a healthy shot of liquor and a cigar.

"I know it's early in the day," Wheeler said. "But I am wounded. It helps the pain."

"It helps all kinds of pain," Slocum replied as he took a sip of bourbon.

"You're looking much better, Father," Rebecca said.

Wheeler smiled at his daughter. "You never were a good liar, Becky. Could you give me a moment alone with Mr. Smith?"

Rebecca gathered up the dinner plates and took them into the kitchen.

Wheeler turned to Slocum. "Did Cooper's herd come to the river this morning?"

"Made it right before I left," Slocum replied. "He had a lot of men driving the herd."

Wheeler sighed. "I'm counting on the men who used to work for me. I hope they won't turn on me. Becky and I have tried to be fair about letting Cooper use our water. However, he seems to want more."

Slocum did not reply. He smoked his cigar. Wheeler poured him another shot of bourbon.

"I don't want to sell to him if I can help it," Wheeler went on, "but the deck is stacked against me. I don't have to tell you that Cooper owns the sheriff and most of the town."

Slocum sighed. "You got any friends in Elkhart?"

"Some. But I was thinking about appealing to the territorial marshal. He might be able to help. Of course, they don't pay us much mind up here in the panhandle. We're not close enough to Oklahoma City."

Slocum looked at him. "Mr. Wheeler, you had somethin' you wanted me to do for you."

Wheeler nodded. "Yes. I'd like you to see Mr. Stewart back to town."

"The lawyer?"

"Do you mind?"

Slocum shook his head. "I work for you. If that's what you want me to do, then I can't argue."

"When you're on the trail, be on the lookout for a wagonload of hay. It should be arriving soon. I want to get it to the herd as soon as possible."

"They need it," Slocum replied.

Wheeler shook his head, sighing. "I hate to see it all go to hell in a hand basket. We need rain bad."

Slocum got up from the table. "That law-reader is gonna need a mount. We can get him to town a lot quicker if he has a horse. The wagon will take twice as long."

"See to it," Wheeler replied.

Slocum thanked him for the meal and the bourbon. As he reached the front door of the ranch house, Rebecca poked her head out of the kitchen to say good-bye.

Slocum just kept going. He did not want to get familiar with the girl. He had enough trouble already.

He went to the stable and chose a mount for the lawyer. By the time the horse was saddled, Stewart was ready to go. The lawyer looked tentative in the saddle, but he managed to hang on.

"I'm not the greatest rider," he told Slocum. "I hail from back East. I never cared much for horses."

They started away from the ranch. Dust stirred around them. Stewart had a frown on his face. Slocum just stared straight ahead. He wasn't exactly looking forward to going into Elkhart.

As it happened, they never made it back to town.

Slocum reined up when he saw the dust rising in the east.

Stewart stopped, too, and looked relieved to get a moment's rest. Then he turned his eyes toward the dust.

"What is it?" he asked Slocum.

Slocum drew his Colt. "I don't know. Stay still until we see."

The lawyer gaped at the weapon. "Is that really necessary? I don't believe in using guns or violence."

"Me either," Slocum replied. "But a lot of other people do."

The dust cloud drew closer. Slocum saw a large wagon coming toward them. It was loaded with bales of dry hay. Slocum holstered his weapon.

The wagon driver reined back when he saw them on the trail. "You point the way to the Lazy River C?" he asked.

"Due west," Slocum replied.

The driver wiped the sweat from his forehead. "I ain't seen it this hot in ten years."

"Get that hay to the ranch as soon as you can," Slocum said. "The herd needs it."

The driver shook the reins. "I'm agoin', pardner. Can't wait to dump this load and get back in the shade."

They watched him go. Then Slocum urged the gray into a walk.

The lawyer had to trot to catch up. "You don't have to be in such a hurry," Stewart complained.

"Sooner I get you back to town, sooner I can get back and help with the herd."

They rode a half mile in silence. Then Slocum heard the shooting. He looked back toward the wagon. A gang of men were attacking. One of them threw a torch onto the hay. The wagon began to burn. Slocum drew his Colt and rode hard toward the fire.

Stewart gaped at the wagon. "Mr. Smith—"

But another shot rang out, and the lawyer fell to the ground, clutching the hole in his chest.

Slocum figured the five men would turn to face him. They did fire off a couple of shots that whizzed by the tall man's head, but when he continued to ride toward them, they turned and ran.

He fired his pistol at them, but the riders were already out of range. They had probably heard about Slocum winging the kid. Why else would they be so afraid of him?

The driver was slumped over on the blazing wagon. A rifle slug had torn a hole in his head. Slocum knew there was only one way to save the rest of the hay. He rode alongside the lead horse of the wagon's team and urged the horses into a gallop. The wagon flew through the hot air and for a moment the flames were fanned by the wind. But Slocum had a plan. He grabbed the lead horse's reins and hauled them quickly to the left. When the team turned, the wagon capsized and broke into pieces as the frightened horses dragged it across the plain, spreading out the hay in a hundred different directions.

Slocum jumped off the gray. He ran toward the flames that still burned. Using his boots, he managed to stomp out some of the fire. The rest of the flames died on their own. His hands were shaking. It had all happened so fast.

The bushwhackers had to be Cooper's men. They had lucked out, finding the hay wagon and the lawyer together. Slocum had no way of knowing which one they had been after in the first place.

He walked back toward the lawyer, who lay still on the ground. The bullet had taken his life. There was nothing more for Slocum to do but catch the horses and take the bodies back to the ranch.

When Wheeler heard horses enter the yard, he came to the door of the ranch house, a puzzled look on his face. Slocum explained what had happened. Wheeler's face turned white. He gaped at the bodies that were lying on the team horses.

"You say that you saved some of the hay?" Wheeler asked.

Slocum nodded. "Somebody's got to tell the sheriff about this. Not that it'll do any good."

Rebecca had followed her father out to the ranch house porch. She wrung her hands and wailed, "There's no hope for us now."

Slocum lowered his head. "Maybe not."

Wheeler looked at him. "You want out?"

Slocum shook his head. "Not yet."

"Get Freeman," Wheeler said. "Take the buckboard and bring back as much of that hay as you can. In the meantime, I'll try to think of a way to get word to the territorial marshal."

Slocum started for the bunkhouse. He felt bad for the Wheelers. But he knew that good people often got a bad shake. It was the way of the West. The law didn't mean much to most men. They just did what they had to do, even if it was wrong.

Slocum went to the bunkhouse to rouse Freeman.

"What's wrong?" Freeman asked.

Slocum told him about the attack on the hay wagon. "Got the lawyer, too," he said.

Freeman shook his head. "Let's go."

They hitched up the wagon and drove back to the mess on the plain.

They pitched most of the good hay onto the back of the buckboard. It was hot working in the sun. Slocum kept watching for the riders to return, but they never did.

"You really think it was Cooper's men?" Freeman asked.

"Who else?" Slocum replied.

Freeman squinted at him. "Why didn't they get you?"

Slocum saw the suspicion in Freeman's eyes. "They didn't have to shoot me, Freeman. Once they got the lawyer and set the hay on fire, I really didn't matter to them."

"No, I s'pose not."

When the hay was loaded, they started back to the ranch.

They passed the ranch house without stopping. The Wheelers waved to them as they rolled toward the herd. They wanted to get the hay to the animals before dark.

Slocum whipped the horse when he saw Cooper's cattle on the banks of the Cimarron. The kid stared at them as they went by. Slocum wondered if the kid had led the raid on the wagon.

"He's surprised to see us," Freeman said with a chortle.

Slocum just kept his eyes forward. He was watching for Henderson. He waved when he saw the trail boss riding toward him.

"I see the hay got here," Henderson said. "What happened to it?"

Freeman related the tale of the attack on the wagon.

Henderson gaped at Slocum. "You all right?"

"I got lucky," Slocum replied. "I managed to turn the wagon over. That was the only thing that saved the hay."

"Good job," Henderson replied. "Come on, let's spread the hay for these critters. It's liable to keep them alive for another day or two."

"You and Bick go on in," Slocum said. "I think Miss Wheeler is expectin' you for dinner."

"What about me?" Freeman asked.

"We'll save you some," Henderson replied.

The trail boss looked at Slocum. "You sure you're gonna be all right out here, Smith?"

Slocum gazed toward Cooper's herd. "Boss, I'm not sure of anything. How about you?"

Henderson tipped back his hat. "I hear you, pardner."

Henderson and Bick rode back toward the ranch.

Slocum and Freeman started to spread the hay. The cattle nosed in to get a bellyful. Some of them nibbled at the bales before Slocum could break them open.

"They're hungry," Freeman said.

Slocum kept looking toward Cooper's cattle. The sun was sinking lower in the west. It would be dark soon. He wondered if the rival rancher had any more tricks up his sleeve.

"Look," Freeman said, "somebody's coming."

Dust was rising in the east.

At first, they thought some of Cooper's men were coming to bushwhack them again. But it was only Henderson and Bick returning. They had food for Freeman. Henderson also had something for Slocum.

"Miss Rebecca sent you this," Henderson said.

Slocum unwrapped a piece of chocolate cake that had been folded in a cloth napkin.

"I think she's sweet on you, Smith," Henderson said.

Slocum glared at him. "I won't have that kind of talk."

Henderson frowned. "Sorry."

Slocum started to eat the cake. He shared it with the others. They were all nervous. Fires burned in Cooper's camp.

After a while, Slocum and the others checked their weapons, readying themselves for another inevitable attack.

8

Slocum opened his green eyes. The sun was rising in the east, casting its rays over the herd. Cooper's men had not attacked during the night. Slocum could see the other camp through the dusty air.

Henderson was hunkered by the campfire. "They're still out there," he said. "They left us alone last night."

Slocum stood up. His body was sore from sleeping on the ground. He stretched, wishing he had some coffee.

"Bick and Freeman are still riding herd," Henderson said. "They're plumb scared to death."

"You blame 'em?" Slocum replied.

"No, can't say as I—uh oh, we got a visitor."

Henderson pointed to the rider that approached from the east. The horse followed the winding bank of the Cimarron. Slocum reached for his Colt. Then he saw the rider was a woman.

Rebecca Wheeler reined back on a small pinto. "Good morning, gentlemen."

Slocum looked away.

Henderson tried to smile. "Miss Wheeler, you shouldn't be out here by yourself."

Rebecca laughed. "I've ridden this range since I was five years old, Mr. Henderson."

"Yes, ma'am. What can we do for you?"

"I've come for Mr. Smith," Rebecca replied.

Slocum glanced up at her. "Me?"

"Father has another task for you."

Slocum looked at Henderson.

Henderson nodded. "Go on. Better'n stayin' here."

Slocum exhaled defeatedly. He was getting tired of being moved around like a piece on a checkerboard, but he had to obey Wheeler. It was part of paying off the debt.

Slocum saddled the gray. Rebecca watched him. He had seen the look before. Sometimes women would get attracted to a man who ignored them. Slocum wanted to avoid the entanglements that came with such an attraction. He climbed into the saddle.

Rebecca turned her pinto and started east.

Slocum spurred the gray. He stayed several yards behind her. He had to eat the dust from the pinto, but he still kept his distance from the woman.

As they passed the Cooper herd, a rider broke away from the cattle. He came over the Cimarron and rode straight for them. Slocum recognized the kid right away.

The kid pulled even with Rebecca. "Howdy, Miss Wheeler," he called.

Rebecca reined back on the pinto.

Slocum trotted up and reached for his gun.

The kid held up his hands. "Hey, I ain't lookin' for trouble."

Rebecca glared at him. "Oh, no? Then why did you shoot my father?"

"He came into the saloon with a rifle," the kid replied. "I didn't have nothin' personal agin' him."

Slocum's eyes narrowed. "Kid, ride back to your herd. I don't want to shoot you."

"What'd I do?" the kid asked. "I didn't—"

"You didn't have anything to do with the attack on our hay wagon?" Rebecca cried.

"No, I was here all the time."

"Sure you were," Slocum replied. "Your boys would lie for you."

The kid glared at him. "You and me are gonna do it one day, Reb. As soon as my hand heals."

Rebecca stiffened proudly in the saddle. "Go back to your employer," she said. "Tell Cooper that my father and I will never give in. Do you hear me? Never!"

She spurred the pinto east again, leaving the kid in a cloud of dust.

The kid shook his head. "I surely like that woman. You got to admire a girl with spirit."

"Take a good look at her," Slocum said. "That's as close as you'll get."

"Don't bet on it, Reb."

"She won't ever forgive you for shooting her father."

The kid grinned. "Women have forgiven men for worse."

Slocum spurred the gray, galloping through the dust left by the pinto. He caught up with Rebecca after a few minutes. She slowed her mount to a walk.

"I hate him!" she said. "He's too familiar. My father went looking for him because he was always bothering me." Tears streaked her pretty face.

Slocum looked away. He didn't want to see her cry. But what could he do about it?

When they arrived at the ranch house, Wheeler was waiting for them in the dining room. He told Slocum to sit down. Rebecca served them a hot breakfast of eggs, grits, biscuits, and gravy. Slocum filled his belly.

"I want you to take those bodies into town today," Wheeler said. "Somebody has to report this to the sheriff."

Slocum nodded.

"No complaints?" Wheeler asked.

"It's your ranch. Like I said—"

"I know, I know. You work for me. I suppose I should be grateful for your dedication, but you don't seem too happy to be here."

"Would you be happy?" Slocum asked.

"No—no, I don't suppose I would."

Slocum got up from the table. "I'll see to those bodies."

He strode out of the house.

The dead men were lying in the stable. Slocum strapped them over the team horses that had pulled the hay wagon. As he was tying the last knot, Rebecca came into the stable.

"John?"

Slocum turned to face her.

Rebecca ran to him and threw her arms around him.

Slocum tensed.

Rebecca buried her face in his chest. "Hold me. Please, just for a moment. I want to—"

Slocum pushed her away. "Get back to the house," he told her.

"But—"

"Don't get any notions, Miss Wheeler."

"I need someone," she said. "I feel so lonely. I need someone to talk to. Someone to share my grief."

"You don't pay me for that."

He turned away, toward the gut-slung bodies.

"How did you become so hard, Mr. Smith?"

"You don't want to know, lady. You just don't want to know."

Slocum led the horses out of the stable. It hurt him to leave her crying. She deserved better.

He told himself that the Wheelers weren't his kin. He worked for them. He couldn't let himself get involved.

He mounted the gray and started to lead the team horses toward Elkhart.

All the way to town Slocum kept waiting for an ambush. He kept a careful watch in all directions. But there were no bushwhackers waiting for him on the plain.

He attracted a lot of attention as he rode into town. The sheriff came out to greet him. Peters gawked at the bodies.

Slocum dismounted and tied all the horses to the hitching post.

"What happened?" Peters asked.

Slocum pointed toward the office. "Inside."

They walked into the office. Peters sat down behind his desk. Slocum sat in a wooden chair.

Before they could start talking, a deputy appeared at the door. "Hey, Mr. Peters, the lawyer's dead. And the other one is that hay driver that come through here."

Peters waved him out.

Slocum started to roll a cigarette.

"What do you know about all this?" Peters asked.

Slocum looked straight at him. "You prob'ly know more'n me."

Peters frowned. "How so?"

Slocum lit his cigarette. "Who wanted that lawyer dead? Who wanted the hay wagon burnt?"

"I don't know," the sheriff replied.

"You don't know because Cooper pays you not to know."

Peters turned red. "Now, just a minute!"

"The wagon was attacked by Cooper's men," Slocum went on. "He didn't want that hay to get to Wheeler's cattle."

"Yeah? Why not?"

"You know," Slocum replied. "He wants the Lazy River spread because the Cimarron runs straight through it. He wants all that water for himself, even after the Wheelers let him water his cows there."

"That's some mighty strong accusations, Smith. You got somethin' to back them up?"

"He wanted the lawyer dead, too. So his men got lucky. I was taking the lawyer to town when they attacked."

"Maybe you killed both of 'em!" Peters said. "You were there."

"I was. But I saved that wagonload of hay. I wasn't fast enough to save the two men."

Peters eyed the tall man from Georgia. "What kind of hand are you playin' in all this, Smith?"

"A bad hand. Only I got to stay at the table because I owe the Wheelers."

"You're wrong," Peters said. "Cooper wouldn't do what you said. He ain't that kind."

Slocum chortled. "No?"

Peters rubbed his chin. "No, he wouldn't."

Slocum stood up. "Peters, the Cooper herd is out there right now, watering at the Cimarron. There's gonna be more trouble. You know it, even if you won't admit it."

Peters shook his head. "It ain't no lookout of mine. That's out of my jurisdiction."

"Then get the marshal down here," Slocum replied. "He can help the Wheelers. Somebody's got to protect them from

Cooper, and you sure as hell aren't doing it."

Peters got up and slammed a fist on his desk. "I s'pose you're gonna protect 'em."

"No, I'm just a hired hand. If trouble comes, I'll use my gun. But I'm not a lawman."

"There won't be no trouble," Peters insisted.

Slocum scowled at the sheriff. "What happens when the range war starts? You gonna go out there and bury the Wheelers? Or you gonna stay here and draw your wages?"

"Get out of my office!"

Slocum turned and walked away. He pushed through the people who were gawking at the dead bodies.

Someone grabbed his shoulder. "Mr. Smith?"

He turned to glare at Thornton, the blacksmith. "What the hell do you want, Thornton?"

The smithy frowned. "I was just wonderin' how the Wheelers were doin'."

"Bad."

Slocum grabbed the reins of the gray. He started down the street. Thornton followed him.

"Do they need hands?" Thornton asked.

"They need more'n that," Slocum replied. "Most of their men walked out to work for Cooper."

"Damn that Cooper!"

Slocum turned to look at Thornton. "If it wasn't for you losing my horse, I wouldn't be in this mess."

"I want to help," Thornton said. "I like the Wheelers."

"Then get a gun. Meet me at the banks of the Cimarron. We'll see how bad you want to help."

"The Cimarron?"

"Both herds are watering there," Slocum replied. "There's going to be trouble. Maybe a range war. And the Wheelers will lose the battle." Slocum swung into the saddle.

"Wait for me," Thornton said.

"You catch up if you really want to help."

Slocum spurred the gray west. As he galloped toward the Lazy River C, he considered leaving the Oklahoma territory. What good would he do against Cooper's men? If Cooper had no conscience about killing the lawyer and the wagon driver, he surely would not worry about murdering everyone at the Wheeler place.

But Slocum kept on. He didn't feel right about running out. Maybe he was sweet on the girl. Maybe he just wanted to get himself killed.

"Smith!"

He reined the gray and looked behind him.

Thornton loped toward him on a tall chestnut mare. Slocum waited for the smith. When Thornton drew closer, Slocum saw that the brawny man was wearing a side arm. He also had a rifle on his saddle.

Thornton touched the Colt on his hip. "I'm signin' on, just like you said."

Slocum sighed and shook his head. "You sure you want to do this?"

"I'd go a long way to defend the honor of Miss Rebecca."

"Yeah."

Slocum turned the gray west again. He eased the animal into a walk. Thornton rode beside him.

"How bad is it, Mr. Smith?"

"You ever hear of the Little Big Horn?" Slocum asked.

Thornton swallowed. "Yes, I have."

"Make your own guesses."

"Cooper ain't Custer, is he?"

"Nope."

"Well, I don't care. I want to help out."

"Go back to town," Slocum replied.

"Why would you say that?"

"Because, if I say it now, I won't feel so bad when I see your dead body lying on the ground."

But Thornton could not be dissuaded, so Slocum just spurred the gray into a lope. The blacksmith stayed right beside him. They rode on to the Lazy River C.

As they approached the ranch house, Slocum saw Wheeler standing on the front porch.

"Thornton's hiring on," Slocum told the rancher.

Wheeler frowned. "I can't pay you, son."

"I don't care," Thornton replied. "I want to help you, sir."

"Much obliged," Wheeler said.

Rebecca came out onto the porch. "Father, is—? Oh, it's you." She frowned at Slocum.

Thornton smiled. "Howdy, Miss Rebecca."

She went back into the house.

"How'd it go in town?" Wheeler asked.

"How you think?" Slocum replied. "Peters says this isn't his jurisdiction. You can't count on him."

Wheeler eyed the tall son of Dixie. "What about you, Smith? Can I count on you?"

"For another twenty-three days," Slocum replied. "After my debt's been worked off, you're on your own."

9

The sun did not let up on the Lazy River C. Days, then weeks of hot weather extended the drought into the heart of summer. Slocum counted the days, marking time as he rode herd on the Wheelers' cattle.

The hay lasted a while, but it finally disappeared. The river also shrank, leaving only a narrow band of water for the dogies. Their noses dipped into the mud as they drank. Slocum wondered how much longer the herd would stay alive.

Each day he counted one or two less steers. Still, the herd was well over four hundred animals, even as some of them dropped in the heat. The Wheelers had a chance if the rains ever arrived.

But the sky stayed clear. Slocum looked for clouds every morning, but rain never came. A dry, hellish wind rolled in from the west, stirring dust into whirling devils. It sent Thornton back to town. He just gave up.

Henderson would begin every day with the same statement: "Dust storm weather. Hope we don't get caught in one."

Cooper's herd also stayed on the Cimarron. The steers watered in the river just like Wheeler's herd. Cooper's cattle were also dying. But the hostile cowhands never made a move against Slocum and the others.

Slocum had figured that the kid would come after him sooner or later. He knew the kid's hand was healing. He could see him in the afternoons, practicing his quick draw.

But there were no problems with Cooper's men. In fact, they shared some of the hay that arrived on a big wagon.

The kid himself dragged several bales to Wheeler's starving cattle. It was an unexpected gesture that made Slocum even more suspicious.

Henderson told the tall man from Georgia not to question the move. The hay kept the steers alive. It was an even trade: hay for water. Cooper was only doing the right thing for a change.

Slocum still kept a close eye on the kid and the other wranglers who rode for Cooper. He knew that they wouldn't have a chance against the superior numbers. Slocum wanted to run if he had to get away in a hurry.

The tall man slept very little during the night. Henderson had given him a rifle, so he always had the Winchester at his side. He could see the campfires from Cooper's men. They were always there, like coyotes waiting for a mountain lion to leave a fresh carcass.

Cooper had to make a move. He had not given up. He had worked too hard killing the lawyer and destroying the hay wagon.

Maybe Cooper had something else in mind. But what? If he wasn't going to ride against Slocum and the others, he was probably waiting for Wheeler to turn belly up like a dead fish in the Cimarron.

Slocum could only keep his rifle next to him as he counted the days.

"Three weeks," Henderson said at the beginning of another hot day. "You almost done your time, Smith."

Slocum nodded. He stood up, stretching. He had four more days left before his obligation to the Wheelers was over.

"You really gonna leave?" Henderson asked.

Slocum did not reply. He gazed to the east, where dust rose in the air. It was probably Wheeler. He had recovered enough to ride. Every other day he brought food to the wranglers.

"It's the girl," Henderson said.

Rebecca Wheeler loped toward them on the small pinto.

Slocum started for his gray. "I'll relieve the other boys."

He saddled the horse, mounting up just as she rode into camp.

Slocum rode away without looking at her. He had been able to avoid Rebecca for almost three weeks. It would make leaving a lot easier.

He had decided to take the gray with him. He figured he had earned it. Wheeler probably wouldn't say anything. The gray was worth a lot less than the wagon of hay that Slocum had saved.

Bick and Freeman saw him coming.

They nodded and rode back to camp. They did not speak to Slocum. Both of them had figured out that the grim Southerner was not much for gab.

Slocum eased the gray into a walk. He looked out over the herd. Walking skin and bone on the hoof. But they were still hanging on. Life didn't throw it in so easily.

Another steer dropped dead.

Slocum looked away. It was a losing battle. He had to retreat, like his old regiment, retreating from the Yankees.

His green eyes glanced back toward camp.

Rebecca was looking at him. Her head was held high. She knew he was going to desert her.

He looked at the cows again.

Rebecca was there, ready for him, but he would not take it. A man didn't always follow the easy road. It boiled down to doing the decent thing once in a great while. Then it would be balanced off with the next indecent act.

He remembered the last woman he had been with. Belle had picked his pockets. But the memory was almost worth it. Almost.

He sighed when Rebecca rode away on the pinto.

Henderson came out to give him some corn bread and molasses. Rebecca had also brought coffee, but Slocum would have to go back to camp for it. Henderson couldn't steady hot coffee in his saddle.

"That girl always asks about you," Henderson said to the tall man.

"And I always tell you I don't want to hear it."

Henderson sighed. "Never could understand you hard cases."

"Get too close to the flame, you burn. I've been burned enough, Henderson. Now I'm cold."

"Hard to be cold in this swelter. Dust storm weather. Hope we don't get caught in one."

Slocum gazed toward Cooper's herd. "There's your dust storm. It just hasn't decided to blow right now."

Henderson swallowed. "You still think there's a chance they'll ride against us?"

"There's always that chance."

That evening, Wheeler rode out to camp. He arrived on a black stallion that galloped with the smoothest gait that Slocum had ever seen. Wheeler dismounted by the fire and took out a bottle of whiskey.

All four men were by the fire. Wheeler filled their tin cups with the sweet liquor. After they drank, Wheeler told Bick and Freeman to go on night herd a little early.

When they were gone, Wheeler handed a leather pouch to Henderson. "Some wages for you and the boys. Not much. Seven dollars for Bick and Freeman. Ten for you, Henderson."

Henderson frowned. "You sure you can spare it, Mr. Wheeler?"

Wheeler nodded. "I sold some things."

"To Cooper?"

"Yes. I wanted to give you something. You men have stuck with me through this ordeal. You have something coming to you."

Henderson looked at Slocum. "What about John?"

Wheeler glared at the tall man. "His debt will be paid in a few days. I figure he'll be leaving us."

"You figure right," Slocum replied.

Wheeler held out a pouch to Slocum. "Here's something to help you along, Mr. Smith."

Slocum shook his head. "I can't take it."

"But you—"

"I thought I'd keep the gray," Slocum said.

Wheeler shook his head. "If that's what you want."

Slocum figured that Wheeler had offered him the money to make him stay.

Wheeler stood up, gazing toward Cooper's herd. "I think it worked out for the best, anyway. Things are peaceful."

"For now," Slocum said.

Wheeler frowned at him. "Explain yourself, sir."

Slocum shrugged. "Cooper's doing just like you. He's waiting. He's tried a few moves that fell short. But he's not going down, he's not losing everything. If he wanted the Lazy River C once, he still does. He might try to take it again."

Wheeler disagreed. He said the sheriff had probably warned Cooper to lay off. The marshal had even paid a visit to the rancher.

"I hope you're right," Slocum replied.

Wheeler gave them another drink before he left. Then he mounted up and rode away in the twilight.

"Good man," Henderson commented.

Slocum just looked into the fire. The whiskey had made him start thinking about women. He saw Belle, naked under him. She had wanted it so bad. Then she had picked his pocket afterward.

"When you plannin' on pullin' out?" Henderson asked him.

"Four days. Maybe three."

"You don't feel bad about leavin' us?"

Slocum chortled. "Does a man feel bad about getting out of prison?"

"Sometimes you have to do somethin' for a good reason," Henderson offered.

"Yeah, but I'm about at the end of my good reasons. I stuck with the deal. I paid my debt to the Wheelers."

"You did. Many other men woulda ridden out."

"I'm going to," Slocum replied. "And you probably won't even see me go."

Henderson stood up. "Think I'll go out with the cattle. Them steers make better company."

Slocum ignored the slight. The tall man knew it was time to leave soon. He stared into the fire as Henderson rode away.

Slocum wanted to feel some regret, but somehow the feeling would not surface in his heart.

The tall man from Georgia opened his eyes. He stood up in the darkness. The twenty-five days had elapsed. He could leave the Lazy River C.

Henderson snored in his bedroll.

Slocum quietly gathered his gear. He found the gray and saddled up. The horse snorted as Slocum mounted, but Henderson did not awaken.

Slocum turned the gray east. He figured to follow the near bank of the Cimarron for a while. He wanted to get around Cooper's herd before he turned north. He hoped he could get away from the drought by riding toward the high country. His empty pockets would be a problem until he found work.

The cool air was dusty and stale.

Slocum rode through the darkness, following the river. He could hear and smell Cooper's herd. It felt good to be leaving them for the last time. Like pulling out a deep splinter.

When he had cleared the herd, he crossed the Cimarron. The gray's hooves were barely dampened by the stream. What would happen if the river finally dried up? Slocum didn't care. He wouldn't be there when it happened.

He turned the gray to the north. It was better if the old man and the girl lost the ranch. The dirty borderland of Oklahoma was no place for Rebecca.

Slocum rode hard for a half hour and then slowed the gray to a walk. He figured he had gotten far enough from the Cimarron. At least until he heard the horse coming behind him.

The dark rider was on Slocum before he could get the gray back into a run. He pulled his gun, but he never fired.

Rebecca Wheeler had caught up with him on her father's black stallion. "I knew you would run," she said. "I knew it."

"I squared our deal."

"Yes. And then you run like a Johnny Rebel coward!"

That cut him deep. Slocum turned away, easing his mount to the north.

Rebecca followed him. "Why can't you stay?"

He didn't want to tell her that the Lazy River C was almost sunk.

"My father needs you!" she cried.

Slocum did not reply.

Suddenly the gray started to limp.

Slocum dismounted and pulled a rock from its hoof.

Rebecca jumped down beside him. "John, please don't go." She threw her arms around him.

Slocum pushed her away. "Don't do this to me."

"To you! What about our ranch?"

"I can't stay."

She grabbed him again, pressing her lips to his.

Slocum let himself kiss her. He drank from her lips. She tasted sweet and tender. He hadn't kissed a woman iike her for a long time. Pain swelled inside him. He pushed her away.

"I love you," Rebecca said.

"No, you don't."

She tried to kiss him again, but Slocum would not let her. "Go home, girl."

"I hate you! You coward!"

Slocum swung into the saddle of the gray.

Rebecca continued to shout at him, but he started away. He wondered if she would follow. He wondered if he should stay and take advantage of her. He had done worse in his time.

"I hate you!" she cried again.

Slocum spurred the gray into a lope. He knew she could catch him on the stallion. But Rebecca did not come after him. When he finally looked over his shoulder, she was riding back toward the Lazy River C.

Slocum ached inside, but he knew he had to keep going. Maybe the hurt would stop by the time he reached Cheyenne.

He could find work in Cheyenne, even if it was just shoveling shit. Of course, that meant going through Colorado by living on whatever he could shoot on the trail. He still had the rifle Henderson had given him. He could plug rabbits or a small deer.

The sun rose to his right as Slocum guided the gray between two mounds of earth. He came over a rise. The ground sloped downward and then leveled off onto a flatter plain.

Slocum had ridden another half mile when the riders appeared. They came from both sides. Ten of them surrounded him.

Slocum recognized the Cimarron Kid as one of the riders.

They were Cooper's men.

The kid rode up beside him. He took Slocum's rifle from the scabbard. Then he reached for Slocum's side arm.

10

The Cimarron Kid seemed to be in charge of the riders. Slocum had never heard of the kid before he came to Oklahoma. Every territory had its local guns for hire. Slocum had to wonder if the kid's gun hand had healed yet.

The horses kept pounding the dusty plain. They were riding due north.

At least Cooper's men had not killed Slocum. Maybe the head man wanted him alive for a while. Maybe he wanted to hang Slocum over the fire, torture him first.

The kid reined up when he saw the wagon on the trail ahead of them. The other riders stopped. Somebody took the reins of Slocum's gray and yanked it to a halt.

Slocum glared at the gunman. But he could not make a move. There were too many men around him. Even if he broke for it, somebody would get him with a rifle shot.

The kid gave directions to the driver of a big hay wagon. Cooper had ordered another load for his cows. It was the only way to keep them alive during the drought.

The hay wagon moved on.

Slocum scowled at the kid. "Cooper gonna share that load with the Wheelers' herd?"

The kid smiled. "Since when did you get so righteous, Reb? Wasn't you runnin' out on Becky and her daddy?"

"Leave her out of this, Kid."

"I can't, Reb. Becky is what this is all about."

The kid spurred his mount into a gallop.

The others followed. Slocum found himself being led north.

They covered a lot of ground before Slocum saw the gate to the Cooper Cattle Company. They rode under a large arch made of saplings. Slocum saw the ranch house in the distance. There was also a stable and a bunkhouse, just like the Wheelers' place.

Most of the men split off from the group, making for the bunkhouse. The kid took the reins of Slocum's mount. He led the gray toward the ranch house. There were two men sitting on the porch with shotguns. One of them looked up at Slocum. "Where'd you find him?"

"He was trespassin' on Mr. Cooper's land," the kid replied. "He's the reb that's been workin' for Wheeler."

"The one who shot you, Kid?"

"Same one."

The man smiled at Slocum. "You're lucky to be alive, Reb." He turned to the kid. "How come you didn't kill him?"

"Shut up! Just shut your damned mouth," the kid snapped.

The other man grimaced, but he held his tongue. He was afraid of the kid. It showed in his face. Mabye the kid's gun hand had healed already.

The kid dismounted. "Get down, Reb."

Slocum climbed out of the saddle.

"Put your hands behind your back," the kid said.

Slocum hesitated.

The shotguns turned on him.

Slocum had to obey.

The kid tied his wrists together. He pushed Slocum, who stumbled forward onto the porch. One of the men stuck a shotgun in his stomach.

"I could get him now, Kid."

Sweat broke over Slocum's face.

"Don't shoot," the kid replied. "Cooper wants to see him."

Slocum wasn't sure he liked the sound of that.

The man drew the shotgun barrel away. "Looks like it's your lucky day, Reb. Less'n the kid is savin' you for hisself."

The kid took Slocum's arm. "Come on, fool. Your luck is bound to run out sooner or later."

He took Slocum into the ranch house. It wasn't as fancy as Wheeler's place. The walls were dark and dusty.

The kid ushered him down a long hallway. He opened a door, pushing Slocum into a room that seemed brighter than the rest of the house. The kid told him to sit in a wooden chair.

"How can I sit with my hands tied?" Slocum asked.

"Then stand," the kid replied. "See if I give two hoots in hell."

The kid slammed the door, leaving Slocum alone in the room.

For a moment, the tall man entertained notions of escape. He could dive through a window. He would have to get his hands loose first.

The door opened again. A stocky man came in. He was wearing a dark suit. He looked rough. He peered at Slocum.

"My name is H. L. Cooper. I'm glad to meet you."

He extended his hand.

"I can't shake," Slocum replied. "I'm hog-tied."

Cooper glanced out into the hall. "Jimmy, get in here and cut this man loose."

The kid came in, smiling sheepishly. "Sorry, Mr. Cooper. I didn't want to take any chances." He cut Slocum's bonds.

"You can leave now, Jimmy," Cooper said.

The kid glared at Slocum and then made his exit.

Cooper offered Slocum a chair. "Sit down, Mr. Smith. John Smith, isn't it? At least that's what I've heard."

Slocum eased down into the chair. "Call me what you want."

Cooper sat down behind a desk. He produced a bottle of whiskey. He poured two shots and pushed one toward Slocum.

Cooper knocked back the shot. "Go on, drink. It isn't poisoned."

Slocum downed the shot. It was smooth. Cooper liked to drink expensive whiskey. The rancher poured himself another.

Slocum thought Cooper looked tired. He hadn't expected such a rough-looking character. Cooper's hands had the calluses of a working man.

Cooper ran a palm over his slicked-back hair. He had some gray mixed in with the black, which framed a sun-worn face and neck. If he hadn't been wearing the fancy suit, he could have passed for a cowboy.

Cooper glanced sideways at Slocum. "Bad business, this drought. It's costing me a fortune."

"It's costing everybody," Slocum replied.

"You mean the Wheelers. You were working for them, weren't you?"

Slocum did not reply.

Cooper sighed. "You're right, the cursed drought is hurting everyone. But that's the way of the West. One suffers, we all suffer. Sure, some suffer worse than others. That's called survival."

Slocum held his tongue. He did not want to get Cooper angry at him. So far the rancher had been reasonable.

"Why aren't you working for the Wheelers anymore?" Cooper asked.

Slocum shrugged. "I owed them. I worked off my debt. Now I'm free to go. I'm going."

"Just like that?"

Slocum nodded. "I reckon."

Cooper stood up. He looked out the window. Slocum thought about taking him right then. He could knock him out and then escape through the window. Of course, he'd have to face every hand on the ranch after that.

"I worked hard for this ranch," Cooper went on. "I came here twenty years ago. We still had Indian trouble back then. But a man could take what was his. And if he could hold it— Well, I've held it this long. Survived the war. And I'll survive this drought." He turned back to look at Slocum.

The tall man wondered if the Yankee rancher was going to kill him.

"I want to hire you," Cooper said. "Would you like to sign on?"

Slocum frowned. "Hire me?"

"You need a job, don't you? If you worked off a debt to Wheeler, you couldn't have left there with much money."

Cooper was one smart Yankee. He knew he had Slocum over a barrel. If Slocum said no to the job, then Cooper could send the kid after him. Or he could just kill him outright.

"How much was Wheeler paying you?" Cooper asked.

"I told you, I worked off a debt."

"At what wage?"

"Two dollars a day," Slocum replied.

Cooper laughed. "I'll double that."

"Why do you want men?" Slocum asked. "You have more now than you need. I'd just be another hand in your pocket."

Cooper sat down again. He didn't seem that ornery. He leaned back in his chair, studying Slocum.

"I need an answer, Smith," Cooper said.

Slocum looked at the rancher again. "Let me get this straight, Cooper. If I don't sign on with you, am I free to go?"

Cooper smiled. "Yes. But you'll have to face the kid. If you come to work for me, I'll keep him off your back."

"I'm not afraid of the kid."

"No, I don't suppose you are." Cooper leaned forward. "But if you kill the kid, which I wouldn't like at all, then you might leave here and go straight to the marshal."

"I heard the marshal's already been here," Slocum replied. "Besides, I aim to head north to Wyoming."

"Bad up that way," Cooper said. "No work, not even in the mines. No, you'd do better to stay here, Smith."

Slocum thought Cooper had a point. "Do I get to think about it?"

"No, I need your answer now."

Slocum thought the opportunity might be a real one. Cooper wanted to put him on the payroll. But why? Maybe Cooper was afraid of the kid and hoped Slocum would kill him eventually.

"What about it, Smith? Can I count on you?"

"I won't do anything against the Wheelers," Slocum replied. "They were good to me. I could never hurt either one of them."

Cooper smiled. "Sounds like you're sweet on the girl. Is that it, Smith? Don't want to hurt your true love."

Slocum bristled, but Cooper headed him off. "I was just joshing you, Smith. I don't care what you feel for the girl."

"I can't ride against the Lazy River," Slocum repeated. "The Wheelers haven't done anything to me—or to you, for that matter."

Cooper nodded. "You're right. I couldn't agree more."

Slocum eyed him. "You joshin' me again?"

"No. I mean what I say. I don't want to do anything to the Wheelers. No, I need you for another reason."

Slocum leaned back in the chair. "Give me another shot of that whiskey and I'll listen to you."

Cooper filled his glass. "Anything else I can get for you?"

"I could use a smoke," Slocum replied.

Cooper produced a pouch of tobacco and some rolling papers. He watched Slocum twist a cigarette. He even offered a sulphur match to light it.

Slocum smoked, keeping his eye on the rancher. "Is this a last cigarette before the firing squad, Cooper?"

"You still haven't given me an answer."

"Why would you want me to work for you?" Slocum replied. "I shot the kid, stood up for Wheeler. I even bad-mouthed you to the sheriff."

Cooper shrugged. "All water under the bridge."

Slocum wanted to ask Cooper if his men had anything to do with the attack on the hay wagon, but he held his tongue. If Cooper was going to forgive and forget, then there was no reason to push him.

"You still haven't told me why you want to hire me," Slocum said.

"All right. We're going to take the cattle to Abilene. I plan to start this week."

"A trail drive? In this weather? Hell, there won't be any water between here and Abilene."

"We can make it to the Arkansas River," Cooper replied. "Follow the Arkansas west for a while. It won't be too bad."

Slocum shook his head. "I don't know, Cooper. I wouldn't want to get stuck with a herd and no water. You think those cows are strong enough as it is?"

"I just sent a load of hay out there. As soon as they're fed, we can start moving them."

Slocum sighed. "I still don't know."

"I'm offering you a fair wage for a day's work," Cooper said. "I know you've run cattle before. You'd be a fool not to accept my offer."

Slocum knew he was right. Four dollars a day to punch cows. Where was Cooper getting the money?

"What about the sheriff?" Slocum asked. "Can you keep him off my back?"

Cooper frowned. "What makes you think I control the sheriff?"

"What makes you think I'm a fool?"

Cooper laughed. "All right. Peters won't give you any trouble. Nobody will. Is that good enough for you?"

"Yes," Slocum replied. "I'll sign on with you. But you have to promise me you won't do anything against the Wheelers."

"You have my word."

Slocum knocked back the shot of whiskey that Cooper had poured for him. "It's a deal, Cooper."

Slocum figured he was entering into a devil's bargain, something he had done before in his wanderings.

"I'll have the kid show you to the bunkhouse," Cooper said. "Stick close to the ranch. I don't want you on the herd yet."

Slocum agreed that was best. He really didn't want to go back out to the Cimarron. He didn't want Henderson and the others to see him working for Cooper.

"Jimmy!"

Slocum turned toward the door, expecting the kid to enter the office.

But another familiar face appeared out of nowhere. "Mr. Cooper, do you want me to—"

Slocum stood up. "You!"

The man gaped at the tall, green-eyed rebel. "I—"

Slocum jumped for him. He tackled the intruder, shoving him out into the hall. Slocum slammed a fist into the man's gut.

Suddenly, the kid and Cooper were there, pulling Slocum off the man.

"Why'd you go after him?" Cooper asked.

Slocum pointed at Tyler Jensen, the gambler who had stolen all of his money. "This boy and his girlfriend fleeced me while I was in Elkhart. They got me drunk and rolled me."

Cooper glared at Jensen. "That true, Tyler?"

The gambler gawked at Slocum. "He's lying. I never took anything from him. He's lying, I tell you."

Slocum started after him again.

The kid stepped between them. "Easy, Reb. No need to hurt him. You can get it back at the poker table."

"I want my money," Slocum said. "And he's got it."

"I do not!" Jensen cried.

"Then I'm gonna take it out of your hide!"

Cooper stepped between them this time. "That's enough. If you're going to fight, do it outside!"

"Fine by me," Slocum replied. "But he's gonna get it, either way."

Jensen was on the verge of tears. "I tell you, I didn't take anything from him. Never!"

Cooper glared at the gambler. "I caught you trying to sneak out of town. You had a wad of money on you. It could have belonged to Smith."

"No, I—"

"Take them outside," Cooper said.

The kid laughed. "Well, Reb, looks like we got ourselves a fight!"

11

Once they were outside, it didn't take long for the crowd to gather in a circle around the yard. Bets went down. Slocum became the favorite of the wagering. Nobody liked the gambler much. They had all lost money to Tyler Jensen.

Cooper presided over the bout. He stood on the front porch with the kid beside him. The kid kept flexing his gun hand.

"No rules," Cooper said. "It doesn't have to be to the death. A man can give whenever he wants to."

"All right," Jensen said. "I give. I don't want to fight him."

Cooper glared at the gambler. "Jensen, how much did you take him for? Be honest."

"I didn't—"

"Yes you did," Cooper said. "You took every penny he had and you didn't take it at the card table."

Jensen lowered his eyes. "I can't remember how much it was."

Cooper pointed at Slocum. "Then John has a real gripe against you. He's got a right to settle it."

Slocum raised his fists. "Come on, gambler." He started to circle.

Jensen looked up. His eyes were glassy. Without warning, he charged straight at Slocum, trying to tackle him.

Slocum sidestepped Jensen's rush. The gambler fell into the dirt. He squirmed and then jumped up to his feet.

"Get him!" the hired hands cried.

"Kick him!"

"Bite him; there ain't no rules."

Slocum began to stalk Jensen. The gambler was quicker than he looked. He managed to avoid the first few punches.

All of a sudden the hired hands were ready to bet on Jensen.

He tried to tackle Slocum again. The tall man swung a fist down into Jensen's back. Jensen fell again.

"Get up," Slocum said. "Fight like a man."

Jensen got up slowly. They started to circle. Jensen tried to come in with a left hand.

Slocum went over the top with a right. His fist caught Jensen in the face. Jensen staggered backward.

Slocum began to double up his punches. Jensen tried to dodge the blows, but most of them got through. Jensen's head snapped back several times.

Betting stopped again.

Slocum slammed a fist into Jensen's forehead. The gambler went down on his seat. He sat there, his eyes rolling in his head.

"He's had it," someone said.

"No he ain't! Get up, gambler."

"Get that reb."

Jensen stood up again. The men who had wagered on him called their encouragement. Jensen raised his fists.

Slocum came right through them. He threw lefts and rights that staggered the gambler. Jensen hit the dust facedown.

"He's finished," Cooper said.

Slocum gazed at the beaten gambler. It hadn't been much of a fight, but Jensen had been served with his comeuppance.

The betting money changed hands again, this time with payoffs.

Slocum started to turn away.

Someone yelled, "Hey, it's not over. The gambler's getting up."

Cooper nodded at Jensen. "Take heed, Smith."

Jensen was on his feet. He staggered a little. Then he drew a knife out of his coat pocket.

"I'm gonna take you apart, drifter."

Slocum jumped back as Jensen lunged with the blade. He caught Jensen's wrist. Slocum brought up a knee, slamming it into the gambler's groin.

Jensen gave a grunt and dropped the knife.

Slocum stood him up and fired another fist into his face. Jensen went down on one knee. Slocum knocked him on his back.

Jensen reached into his pocket again. Slocum kicked his hand. A pocket revolver flew into the dust.

"You can't shoot me, either," Slocum said. "Now get up, or give up. It's your lookout."

Jensen nodded and spat blood into the ground.

"Say it," Slocum said.

"I give."

Cooper waved at his men. "It's over."

They dispersed as the bets were paid off.

Cooper started into the house.

Slocum called to the rancher. "Mr. Cooper?"

"Yeah?"

"I'm not bunking with the other men," Slocum said. "If you don't mind, I'll sleep in the stable loft."

Cooper sighed. "I see your point. After the fight, some of them might want to try you. Especially after you winged the kid here."

The Cimarron Kid glared at his employer. "You didn't have to say somethin' like that, Mr. Cooper."

The rancher looked at both of them. "Now listen to me, men. I won't have any more nonsense. If you two have a private beef, keep it to yourselves. You can settle it on a Saturday night in Elkhart. Is that clear?"

Slocum nodded.

The kid glanced away. "Whatever you say, Mr. Cooper."

Cooper cast one last look at Jensen. "I don't know why I even kept him here. Or maybe I do." He went into the house.

The kid turned to face Slocum. "I ain't forgot that you shot me in the hand, Smith. I ain't as mad as I once was, but I'm still sore."

Slocum shrugged. "Like Cooper said, we'll save it for Saturday night. Until then, you can give me back my gun."

The kid smiled. "Yeah, I reckon I did take your weapons. I didn't know Mr. Cooper was goin' to hire you then."

Jensen moaned on the ground.

"Shut up," the kid said. "I always knew he was a pantywaist. He almost got you with that knife."

"Almost," Slocum replied. "I want my guns, Kid."

"Call me Jimmy."

Jensen moaned again.

The kid moved to help him up. "Come on, dandy. We'll get you some whiskey and a deck of cards. In a few days, you won't even hurt that bad." He took Jensen into the house.

Slocum turned in a wide circle, surveying the ranch. Some of the other men were looking at him. Slocum was the cock of the walk for now. How long before another gunman came out of the pack to challenge him?

"Smith!"

Slocum turned back toward the house.

The kid was holding his Colt and his rifle. "Here you go, Reb. Don't shoot yourself in the foot."

Slocum took his weapons, inspecting them carefully.

"I didn't do anything," the kid said. "Don't you trust me?"

Slocum's eyes were green slits in the sun. "Tell me you wouldn't like to see me dead."

"I would. But only if I'm shootin' you, Smith. Smith? That's a pretty common name."

"What of it?"

The kid grinned. "That's my name, too. Jimmy Smith."

Slocum turned away, heading for the stable.

"See you on Saturday night," the kid called.

Slocum just kept walking. He wasn't afraid of the kid. But he still wanted to get the hell away from the Cooper Cattle Company.

A dozen pairs of eyes watched him as he entered the stable. It wasn't going to be easy to slip away. Cooper had too many hands.

Why did Cooper want Slocum to stay, anyway?

Or the gambler? What was Jensen's place in all this? He seemed to be useless. Unless Cooper was afraid Jensen would take word outside the territory. If Cooper still had it in mind to move against the Lazy River C, then he had to act in private. He was the king of his own little domain. And Slocum had just become one of the pawns.

The liveryman scowled at him. "What can I do for you?"

"Cooper said I can sleep here in the loft."

"Well, it's his place." The man turned back to his work.

"I was riding a gray," Slocum said. "You know where it is?"

"You'll have it when you need it," the man replied. "Your gear is taken care of. Saddlebags are back there on the fence."

Slocum retrieved his saddlebags. Nothing had been disturbed. He threw the bags over his shoulder and climbed to the loft.

There wasn't much hay to sleep on.

Slocum spread out near the loft door. He wanted to be able to see the yard. He still did not trust Cooper.

Slocum leaned back against the wall of the loft. His hands hurt a little from the fight. If he was around long enough, he still wanted to find a way to get his money back from the gambler.

But the tall man from Georgia figured that running was the best thing. If he could get away from Cooper's men, then he would able to make it to the north like he had planned. That would mean running at night. Pick his moment. Get the hell out of Oklahoma.

He closed his eyes. It was better to rest for a while. He wanted to be strong when he finally moved. He had a feeling that Cooper wasn't going to let him go so easily.

The Cimarron Kid sat in the parlor of Cooper's ranch house with the gambler. "That sure was a sorry display of fisticuffs, Jensen. Your momma teach you how to fight?"

Jensen nodded at the kid's wounded hand. "He got you, too. I don't even know why Cooper's letting him live." Jensen poured himself another cup of brandy.

The kid had a snort himself.

Cooper came in and sat down with them. "Jensen, why don't you leave us now? Go on."

Jensen looked at the bottle of brandy. "I'll need some more of this if I'm going to recover."

Cooper nodded impatiently. "Go on, take it. Anything to get you out of my hair."

Jensen grabbed the bottle. "I'm sorry, Mr. Cooper, I—"

"Just go."

The gambler hurried out of the parlor.

Cooper shook his head. "He couldn't fight his way out of a paper bag. I thought he might have a chance when he pulled that knife."

"What a candy-ass," the kid rejoined.

Cooper glanced sideways at him. "You can take care of him."

The kid nodded. "You're the boss."

"Keep it quiet," Cooper said. "And bury him deep. I don't want anyone digging him up."

The kid leaned forward a little. "What about the rebel?"

"I thought we had that straight."

"Why you lettin' him live? I could take him. Hell, after what he did to me, I'd be right if I shot him in the back."

"Not yet," Cooper replied. "We're sticking to the plan. That rebel walked straight into it. Now he's going to be the scapegoat."

"Yeah, yeah. But he thinks he signed on for a trail drive. What happens when he finds out the truth?"

Cooper reached into his coat pocket. "I thought this might help." He handed the kid a piece of paper.

"What's this?"

"Just read it," Cooper said.

The kid unfolded the paper. "Wanted for robbery. John Slocum. Fifty dollar reward for— Hey, this face looks like the rebel."

"He's wanted south of here, in Texas."

The kid laughed. "This'll surprise him."

"Just show it to him if he gives you any trouble."

"Don't worry," the kid replied. "Mr. John Slocum will do what I tell him from now on."

• • •

Darkness had fallen over the dusty plain. Slocum figured it was time for him to go. He gathered up his belongings and started slowly down the ladder of the loft.

He had to find the gray and his saddle. He wanted to take his own mount. That way no one could accuse him of horse stealing.

Slocum hesitated at the bottom of the ladder. He listened for sounds of the liveryman. It was quiet in the stable. Where was he?

A dinner bell rang in the bunkhouse. It was suppertime. Slocum figured he should hurry. He could run while the others were eating.

He ran to each stall until he found the gray. His saddle was hanging on the stall door. Even if they asked him where he was going, he could always say that Cooper had told him to go back to the Cimarron, to the herd.

The gray startled a little. Slocum had to calm it down. He finally got the saddle on the horse's back.

"You gotta run," Slocum said.

He started to lead the gray out of the stall. His green eyes peered into the shadows. He expected one of Cooper's men to come at him with a gun. Cooper wouldn't even have to explain his death to the sheriff.

The front door was closed on the barn. Slocum looked toward the side door. It wasn't big, but he thought he could get the gray through it. Then his departure would not even be noticed.

He led the gray to the narrow door. The horse's head went through, but the saddle would not clear the passage. It caught on the doorjamb.

"Damn it all."

He backed the gray out of the door. He had to take off the saddle if the horse was going to make it out. Once the gray was free, Slocum would have to resaddle it.

His hands worked quickly on the cinch of the saddle. Sweat dripped off him. He was going to ride on an empty stomach. It didn't matter, as long as he got away. The saddle came off. Slocum started to lead the gray through the narrow door.

"That's no way to take a horse out of a barn."

The voice had come from the shadows.

Slocum reached for his Colt.

A woman laughed. "Mr. Smith, I do declare, the only way you know how to greet a girl is with firearms."

"You!"

Belle stood in front of him with a tray in her hands.

"Of course," she replied cheerily. "Who else around here would bring you supper!"

12

Slocum peered through the shadows at Belle. He could smell her perfume. She might be a good enough reason to stay, at least for a while.

"You won't get a mile if you leave," Belle told him. "Cooper has men surrounding the place. You wouldn't even make it out in the dark."

He put the gray back in its stall and hung up his saddle.

"Smart," Belle said. "You can't escape."

"Looks like you couldn't, either."

"Cooper had men waiting for us at the first stage stop," she told Slocum. "He didn't want us to go."

Slocum stood in front of her. "I whipped Jensen's ass today for takin' my money. What makes you think I won't do the same to you?"

Belle sighed. "I don't know, honey. Maybe you will. But this tray's getting heavy. You want to eat or not?"

Slocum took the tray from her. It was loaded with cold beef and some bread. Slocum began to eat.

"I'm sorry about stealing your money," Belle went on. "That was Tyler's idea. Though I do confess to drugging you."

"What about us doing it? That Jensen's idea, too?"

"No, that was my idea. Tyler slapped me for it. The bruise healed, otherwise I'd show it to you for sympathy."

Slocum handed her the tray. "Why does Cooper want you and the gambler to stay here?"

"He doesn't want us spreading the word of his fame and fortune," Belle said. "When you called the marshal on him—"

"I didn't do that; it was Wheeler."

Belle shrugged. "It doesn't matter. Cooper is spooked. He wants to control as much of this as he can."

"Why's he want me?" Slocum asked.

"For something bad," Belle replied. "But I don't know exactly what he has planned."

"Is he gonna try to hurt the Wheelers?"

Belle frowned. "It's that little Becky Wheeler, isn't it? You've got it bad for her. She's too young for you."

"What do you care? What am I to you?" Slocum retorted.

"Oh, you know how it is with women," Belle replied. "We let you lay on top of us and a little part of us thinks we own you."

"Nobody owns me."

Belle laughed. "Cooper does. He owns it all. And he's gonna own the Lazy River C before it's all over."

Slocum grabbed her arms. "Tell me what you know. What's Cooper got up his sleeve?"

"I don't know," Belle whined. "You're hurting me."

Slocum let go of her. "If that girl gets hurt—"

"I was right, it is the Wheeler girl."

Slocum turned away, heading for the loft.

Belle followed him. "Maybe you can get away from here," she offered. "You're smart."

"Not so's you'd notice," Slocum replied dryly. "I got myself trapped in this mess."

Belle touched his shoulder. "John."

Slocum stopped. He turned to face her. She looked beautiful in the shadows. And the perfume was all around him.

"We can get away," Belle said.

"How?"

"Think of something."

Slocum shook his head. "I can't—"

Belle grabbed his face in her hands. She pulled him down so she could kiss him. Her mouth tasted of brandy.

"I want it," she said.

Slocum looked at her. "Want what?"

"I want you, John. I want you to take me out of here."

Slocum laughed. "So that's it. You're looking for a way to escape from Cooper."

"I want you either way," Belle replied. "But you have to promise that you'll help me if you can."

"Sure," Slocum replied.

He figured they would be even when he broke his promise to her.

"Do you mean it?" she asked.

He nodded. What would it hurt to lie to her? She had already picked him clean. He was only leveling the scale.

Belle pressed her body into his. "Where?"

He pointed upward.

She laughed. "In the loft again. It does seem like the best place."

Belle lifted her skirt. She guided his hand to the hair between her thighs. She was really going to give him a show. It was her way of stacking the deck against him.

"Touch me."

Slocum's fingers played in the hair. Belle thrust forward. He felt the moisture on her lips.

"You make me want it," she whispered.

Her hand grabbed his crotch. She massaged the hardness there. Her mouth kissed him again.

"Cooper might catch us," Slocum said.

She shook her head. "He takes a nap after dinner. I— ohh—"

Belle started to lie back right there on the floor of the stable.

"No," Slocum said. "Up there." He started to climb.

Belle glared at him. "Damn you!" But she followed him anyway. Once in the loft, she started to lie down again.

"No," Slocum said. "You can't just lift your dress. I want you naked. All the way."

Belle smiled. "All right. All the way."

It didn't take her long to drop her clothes. A real professional, Slocum thought. Only this time she wouldn't be able to knock him out with any bogus whiskey.

Belle spread out on the floor of the loft. "Do it."

Slocum leaned back on the hay. "Not yet."

He folded his arms. His reluctance made her crazy. Belle was all over him with her hands. She fumbled with the buttons of his fly and freed his prick from his trousers. Her fingers jerked him up and down. Then she lowered her lips to his cock. Belle's wet mouth slid along the crest of his prick. She didn't suck him for long. Her own needs were aching inside her.

Her naked body straddled him. She knelt down. The head of his cock brushed against the moistness between her legs. She groaned as she sat on him. Her face turned upward. His cock slid deep inside her. Belle worked her hips.

Slocum watched her on top of him. He reached up to touch her breasts.

"I want you on me," she said.

She rolled over, and Slocum slid between her legs. His cock prodded her until she guided him in.

Belle lifted her legs. "As hard as you can make it."

Slocum drove his hips downward. Belle grunted with each thrust. He had never known a woman with more hunger. She wrapped her legs around him and bucked like a wild bronc.

"Deep," she whispered. "Give it all to me. All of it."

Her hands gripped his buttocks.

Slocum felt his desire building to a climax.

"In me," Belle said. "Deep in me."

His prick discharged like a cannon. He held on, feeling her body as it quivered beneath him. Belle grabbed his head and guided his mouth to her nipple. Slocum licked the tight ring.

She ran her hands through his hair. "Take me with you, John. I could love you. I really—"

Slocum put his hand over her mouth. He had heard spurs jangling below him. Someone had come into the stable. An oil lamp glowed in the darkness.

"John?" The man's voice echoed through the stable. "Smith?"

Slocum rolled off her. He put a finger to his lips. Belle nodded. She knew to keep quiet.

"John?"

It was Cooper.

Slocum crawled to the edge of the loft. "Yeah?"

"You sleeping?" Cooper asked.

"Just dozin'. I'm ready if you need me."

"You get something to eat?" Cooper asked.

"Yes, sir."

Someone moved in behind Cooper. Slocum saw the kid and the gambler. The kid had his hand on Jensen's shoulder.

"We're goin' into town, Mr. Cooper. Tyler here feels like gamblin'."

Cooper nodded. "Go on. Just don't be back too late. I want everyone ready to ride an hour before daylight. Is that clear?"

"Clear as hell," the kid replied. "Come on, Tyler. We'll take the wagon."

They moved off toward the rear of the stable. The kid did not even look at Slocum. He kept his hand on Jensen's shoulder as he went.

Cooper pointed at Slocum. "That goes for you too, Smith. You're to be in the saddle one hour before dawn."

"I'll be there," the tall man replied.

Cooper wheeled and went out of the stable.

Slocum crawled back toward Belle. She started to speak. He put his hand over her mouth again.

The kid and the gambler were still outside. Slocum could hear them laughing as they rigged the buckboard. They had been drinking and their voices were slurred.

After the wagon was rigged, they drove off to the south.

Slocum took his hand away from Belle's mouth.

"Where's Tyler going with that idiot?"

"To town," Slocum said. "Didn't you hear?"

Belle shivered. "That kid gives me the creeps."

"I thought you said Cooper takes a nap after dinner."

"He does! Hey, I wouldn't set you up."

"You did once," Slocum replied. "Why not again?"

Her hand caressed his cheek. "John, I'm sorry about that. I just wanted to get away from Cooper. I would have done anything. It was my idea to put the drops in the whiskey. Tyler wanted to hit you on the head, but I wouldn't let him. I like you."

Slocum sighed. He figured that women just couldn't help themselves sometimes. They could change like the wind. And storm just as unexpectedly.

"Maybe you should go back," he told her.

Her hand slid down his chest. She didn't stop until she had his prick in her hand. She began to tug at the limp member.

"I need it again," she said. "Cooper coming like that got me all bothered inside."

He felt himself getting harder.

Belle tried her mouth on him again. She really wanted it. The gambler hadn't been doing his job.

"You lie with Cooper?" Slocum asked.

Her body stiffened. "I don't think that's any of your business, you cowboy bastard! I—oh—"

Slocum touched her wet cunt. Belle shuddered. She moved her hips.

"Inside me," she said.

Slocum started to roll over on her.

"No," Belle said. "Have you ever seen a stallion mount a mare?"

He nodded.

"Then mount me like that."

She got up on all fours. Slocum moved behind her. He prodded her with his cock. It slipped into her ass.

"That hurts," Belle told him.

He finally found her cunt. The head of his prick penetrated her. Belle groaned when he sank it in all the way.

"Hard, honey. Hard as you can."

He shook her for a long time. His aching cock would not release. He finally felt his sap rising. Belle collapsed when he discharged inside her. She fell, rubbing herself, twitching for a moment in the hay.

Slocum reached down, grabbing her hair. He put his mouth close to her ear. Belle grimaced at the darkness.

"What's Cooper got in mind for me, woman?"

"I don't—it hurts!"

"Tell me, or I'll yank out your hair."

"John, please—"

"You stole from me," Slocum said. "Took every red cent I had and never blinked an eye."

Belle squirmed. "It's not like that. It—ow—"

She tried to wriggle out from underneath him.

Slocum fell on top of her. His cock was still hard. It slipped down the crack of her ass.

Belle seemed to relax.

Slocum felt her bung against the head of his cock. He pressed forward.

Belle grunted. "Go on, I want you to do it."

He penetrated her all the way. But after a few seconds, he pulled out. It just didn't feel right.

Slocum rolled off her. "Go back."

Belle sat up. "What about our deal?"

"I'm not taking you with me," Slocum replied. "You do what you have to on your own, but don't count on me."

"I'll tell Cooper that you're going to run away," she threatened.

"I'm not."

"What?"

"I'm going to stick it out," Slocum replied. "If I can't get away tonight, I might as well see the thing through."

"What about me?" Belle asked.

Slocum pointed toward the ladder. "Go on. Just don't do anything stupid and Cooper probably won't kill you."

She crawled toward her clothes. "Some help you are!"

"You had your fun," Slocum said. "Now leave me in peace."

It took her a while to put on the dress in the dark.

When she was finished, she looked at Slocum. "John, I really do like you. I really do."

Slocum sighed. "Sure you do. Now get the hell out of here."

She climbed slowly down the ladder. He heard her footsteps in the yard. She quickened her pace as she neared the house. Slocum wondered what kind of lie she would tell Cooper.

He leaned back on the hay, listening. He was not ready for sleep yet. He wanted to wait a while. He did not have to wait long.

The buckboard came back, rattling behind the barn.

Slocum saw the kid come into the stable. He was alone. The gambler had not returned. Tyler Jensen was dead.

Slocum wondered if the kid had another trick to kill *him*.
He closed his eyes.
It wouldn't come until daybreak.
Slocum would try to be ready.

13

"John?"

A woman's hand touched his face.

Slocum sat up. "Back off me, woman."

"John, Tyler didn't come back. I saw the kid—"

Slocum put his hand on her shoulder. "Go back to the house, Belle."

"Why didn't Tyler come back?" Belle whined.

Slocum couldn't bring himself to tell her that the gambler had dealt his last hand. "Honey, you'll be safe in the house. Just go."

"I'm scared, John."

"What time is it?"

"After four," Belle replied. "I—"

Slocum stood up. Belle grabbed his leg. He shook her off.

"Go back to the house!"

Belle began to cry.

Slocum was shaking. She had slipped up on him while he was in a deep sleep. She could have stuck a knife in his chest and he never would have known it.

He climbed down the ladder. He wanted to get his gray saddled. If he got a jump on them, he might be able to run. He could tell the sentries that he was an advance scout.

The gray didn't give him any trouble. He threw the saddle on and reached for the cinch. Belle came up behind him.

"Go home," he told her.

"Where's Tyler?"

He sighed. "Six feet under."

She began to whimper. Slocum put his arms around her. She grabbed him and hung on tightly.

"Well, well. A couple of lovebirds!"

Slocum looked up to see the kid standing there. He pushed Belle away. Then he squared his shoulders, in case the kid made a move.

The kid grinned at Belle. "Mr. Cooper won't like this."

Belle just pushed past him and ran out of the stable.

"Women," the kid said. "Say, where you goin', Smith?"

"The man gave me orders," Slocum replied. "He said an hour before daybreak. I was just getting ready."

The kid grimaced. "Yeah?"

Slocum watched the kid's gun hand. "You figuring to take me for a ride like you did Jensen?"

"Jensen got drunk in town," the kid replied. "I left him in jail. The sheriff's gonna put him on the stage tomorrow mornin'."

"Sure. And we're leavin' on a trail drive. Right?" He led the gray past the kid.

Outside, the other men were falling into ranks. If they really were going on a trail drive, it made sense to leave before daybreak. They could work in the cool of the morning, until the day got hotter, then move again when the sun went down. They wouldn't lose a lot of strays, because the herd was weak and easy to manage.

But they weren't going on a trail drive. All of the men were armed to the teeth. They were checking their pistols and rifles. This was going to be a raid.

Slocum started to sweat.

"Hey," a man said, "you got any scattergun cartridges?"

Slocum shook his head.

The man moved on, looking for shotgun shells.

The kid came out of the barn. He led a tall roan. When he mounted up, the others also climbed into their saddles.

Slocum mounted up with them. They rode away from the ranch house. Slocum was relieved when they turned toward the Cimarron.

Maybe they really were going to drive the herd north.

Dust whirled behind them as the sun inched over the

horizon. The sky was clear. The hot wind picked up as they moved.

Slocum figured it would be easy to slip away once the herd was on the trail. The kid would never be able to find him. He could head north, where there was a lot less trouble.

The kid raised his hand. They came to a dusty halt. He peered west, toward the herd.

"What are you waiting for?" Slocum called.

The kid suddenly turned his mount to the northeast, heading toward the Wheeler place.

The other riders followed him.

"No!" Slocum cried.

They were moving on the Wheelers.

He spurred the gray, falling in behind the gang.

There didn't seem to be much he could do for the Wheelers, but he was sure as hell going to try to help them.

The kid reined back at the bottom of a slight rise. "Smith, come with me. You others stay behind till I give the signal."

The kid started ahead on the roan. Slocum followed him on the gray. They moved to the crest of the rise. Slocum looked down on the Wheelers' ranch house.

"You can't do this," he told the kid.

The punk grinned at him. "Is that right, Mr. Slocum!" His green eyes narrowed. "What's it to you?"

"A little matter of a wanted poster in Texas. It ain't much of a reward. Fifty dollars for a robbery."

Slocum's hand dropped by his side.

The kid's gun hand was also hanging low. "You want to fight now?"

"What's the deal?" Slocum asked.

"We're grabbin' the girl and her father. Gonna force 'em to sign the Lazy River C over to Mr. Cooper."

Slocum grimaced. "That won't be legal."

"Cooper's the law here," the kid replied. "He's gonna buy it outright. He'll give 'em ten percent of what it's worth."

"Generous soul."

"You in, Slocum? Or do I have to shoot you?"

"What do you want from me?" Slocum asked.

The kid peered toward the ranch house. "I'm givin' you a chance to go in and bring out the girl. Her old man, too."

"Me?"

"You worked with 'em," the kid replied. "The girl was sweet on you. I know, I saw the way she came out to see you on the range."

Slocum looked back down the slope, studying the men who had ridden with him. "What if I don't go in?"

The kid shrugged. "We try to take 'em peaceable, but you never know what will happen."

Slocum wasn't scared by the wanted poster, but he was afraid that the kid might hurt Rebecca Wheeler. He didn't want that to happen.

"What's it gonna be, Slocum?"

The tall man gave a nod. "I'll see what I can do."

"Smart man," the kid replied. "You might just stay alive after all, Slocum. I'll give you thirty minutes, then we're riding in."

Slocum moved slowly in the shadows. He had ridden down to the ranch house. Now he had to find the girl and her father.

He tried the back door. It was open. The Wheelers were trusting souls. He started down the hall.

"Hold it right there!"

Slocum turned to stare down the barrel of a scattergun.

Rebecca Wheeler moved toward him. "What are you doing in my—John?"

Slocum nodded at her. "Mornin', Rebecca."

She dropped the weapon and ran to him, throwing her arms around his waist. "I knew you'd come back."

Slocum pushed her away. "Where's your daddy?"

Rebecca frowned at him. "What's wrong?"

"I need to see your father."

"Tell me what's wrong!"

The tall man sighed. "Rebecca, the Cimarron Kid is waiting out there with a bunch of men. They aim to take you and your daddy and force you to sign the Lazy River C over to Cooper."

She ran to get her father.

Robert Wheeler was still in his robe. "Mr. Smith, what's the meaning of this early morning visit?"

Slocum told him about the kid and the other riders.

"They can't be serious!" Wheeler said.

"Cooper wants your ranch," Slocum replied. "He aims to get it."

"What the devil are you doing here?" Wheeler asked.

"I aim to get you out of this mess if I can." Slocum didn't want to tell Wheeler that he had signed on to ride for Cooper. He figured he was about to quit, anyway, and was going to work for Wheeler again.

"What can we do?" Wheeler asked.

"Get your horses saddled. You've still got about twenty minutes before the kid rides in."

Wheeler nodded and started for the stable.

Slocum slipped up to the window. He stared at the rise to the south. There was no sign of the kid and his men. They had to outrun them.

Slocum looked back at Rebecca. "Is there some place we can hide once we get out of here?"

"We have a hunting cabin about ten miles from here. We haven't used it in years, but I'm sure it's still there."

Slocum looked out the window again. "We'll go there."

Rebecca picked up the shotgun again. "I'll help my father with the horses."

"Hurry!" Slocum drew his gun and looked out the window.

The kid rode back down to the other men.

One of them called to him. "What's goin' on, Kid?"

"Hang loose."

It was a good plan. Cooper had thought of it.

The kid pulled out a pocket watch and looked at the time. Slocum had about fifteen minutes left to live. Then the kid could pay him back for shooting his hand.

"Time for a ladies' social, Kid?" someone asked.

The kid gave the man a hard look. "You boys is mighty spirited on a hot mornin'. Anybody feel like seein' if my hand is healed?"

Nobody wanted to find out.

The kid put the watch in his pocket. He checked his pistol again. His nerves were a little edgy. He hadn't seen a lot of action. His reputation had been built on a killing he had taken credit for a couple of years earlier.

"How long we gonna stay here, Kid?"

"Chew on a brandin' fork," the kid replied. "I'm ridin' up again. I'll give the signal when we're ready. It won't be long."

The kid spurred the roan, ascending to the crest of the ridge. He looked down at the ranch house. A few more minutes.

He went over the schedule in his head. Grab the woman. Kill the father. Kill the rebel.

Slocum had to die last.

The kid wanted to face him. He wasn't even sure he could take Slocum, but he had to try. His reputation wouldn't be anything if he didn't get even with the Southerner.

He looked at the watch again. A few more minutes.

They would burn the house and then make it seem as if Slocum had done the whole thing. Even the marshal would stay off their backs if they staged it right.

The kid checked his gun again. He was ready for Slocum. He held the watch in his hand, waiting as the minutes ticked away.

Slocum looked toward the rear of the house. "Rebecca?"

What was taking them so long? He went out the back way, passing his own mount. He found Wheeler in the stable. The rancher was rubbing down his black stallion. Rebecca already had the saddle on her pinto.

"What're you doin'?" Slocum cried.

"My mount needed brushing. He was dirty."

Slocum grabbed the saddle blanket and threw it on the stallion's back. The horse snorted at him. Slocum put on the saddle, cinching it tight. He didn't have time to fool with any ornery animals.

"Where are we going?" Wheeler asked.

"Your daughter said something about a hunting shack," Slocum replied.

"Good," Wheeler said. "But what do I do after that? Let Cooper run me off my land?"

"You go to the marshal," Slocum replied. "All the way to Oklahoma City if you have to. Get somebody on your side. Hell, you could hang 'em for the death of the lawyer if you could prove it."

"Really?" Rebecca said.

Slocum nodded. "I think they killed the gambler, too. If you can dig him up— Well, I don't know."

"Will you help us?" Rebecca asked.

"No, ma'am. Not after we get out of here."

Wheeler grabbed the reins of the stallion. "I can find that shack in the dark if I have to."

"What about the other men?" Rebecca asked. "Henderson, Freeman, and Bick are still at the herd."

"Leave 'em," Slocum replied. "They can run if things get hot. Right now, Cooper wants y'all."

He'd want Slocum, too, when he found out that the tall rebel had helped the Wheelers escape.

"No!" Rebecca said.

Slocum looked back. "What's wrong?"

"I think there's something wrong with my horse."

The pinto limped a little.

Slocum bent to check the hoof. "Just a rock. There, we're ready to go. Try to stay behind the house, so they can't see us."

Robert Wheeler went out first. Rebecca was right behind him. Slocum moved past them, making for the gray. But he never reached his mount.

A whooping cry echoed from the ridge.

The kid was riding toward them. The other riders appeared behind him. They all had their guns drawn.

"He's attacking," Rebecca cried.

Slocum grabbed the rifle from his scabbard. He told them to get into the house. "Use any weapons you got," he cried.

Wheeler and Rebecca ran into the ranch house.

Slocum lifted the rifle and quickly fired one shot.

When the onrushing gunmen returned fire, he followed the Wheelers into the house.

14

The kid led the charge against the ranch house.

Slocum dug in behind a window. He poked the barrel of the Winchester through the glass. The rifle erupted at the bushwhackers. They were still out of range.

"Get out of the way," said Robert Wheeler.

Slocum glanced back to see the rancher holding an old Sharps fifty caliber rifle.

"This'll slow 'em down!" Wheeler said.

Slocum moved out of the way.

Wheeler propped up the Sharps, putting the barrel through the broken pane. He took careful aim. When the rifle went off, it almost threw him backward onto the floor.

Slocum saw the roan go out from under the kid. The other men rushed around him. They kept coming, but they had slowed down some.

Slocum thrust his Winchester out of the window again. He began to fire one shot after another. He managed to kill one of the riders before his rifle went empty.

But the shots kept coming and more of the riders fell. Rebecca Wheeler was firing a Winchester out of another window. She levered the weapon like a madwoman.

The riders all stopped and turned back, making for the spot where the kid had fallen.

Wheeler let go another round from the Sharps and a lagging rider fell to the earth.

Slocum gawked at the older man. "You're pretty good with that thing."

"I'm a deadeye."

Slocum looked at Rebecca. "Are you all right?"

"I'm reloading." She tossed him a box of cartridges. "You should be doing the same."

"Yes, ma'am."

Slocum filled up the Winchester. He levered a round into the chamber and added another bullet. Wheeler put a cartridge in the Sharps.

"What are they doing?" Rebecca asked.

Slocum peered toward the kid and his men. "They're licking their wounds. But they'll try again. They weren't expecting anybody to fight back. We did, though."

"Here they come!" Wheeler cried.

The kid tried to lead the charge on another mount.

Wheeler fired the Sharps. The mount fell under the kid. The charge stopped immediately.

"Got 'em," Wheeler said.

The kid waved his men forward.

"They're coming," Slocum cried.

Wheeler fumbled with the breech of the Sharps.

Rebecca aimed her Winchester. "They're getting closer."

Slocum fired his own rifle. The riders shot back. Slugs ripped through the windows.

Rebecca cried out. A bullet had stung her upper arm. Blood poured through her fingers.

Wheeler's cannon went off.

A rider's head disappeared from his body.

The others turned back again. Their rifles had thinned out the gang, but there were still twelve or thirteen of them left.

Slocum moved to help the girl. "It's just a flesh wound. Tear the hem of your dress."

"What?"

Slocum reached down, tearing a strip from her dress. Rebecca did not protest. She wanted the bleeding to stop.

Slocum wrapped the wound and tied off the bandage. "How's it feel?"

"Numb," Rebecca said. Her face was white, but she did not faint.

Wheeler moved next to his daughter's side. "We've got to get out of here. We can't hold them off forever."

Slocum agreed. "I can carry her to the horses. We can make a break. If we outrun the kid and his men, then we're home free."

"I want to fight," Rebecca said bravely.

"The man is right," Wheeler replied. "Go on. I'll fire one more shot with this rifle and then follow you."

Rebecca tried to stand, but she was too weak. Slocum lifted her in his arms. He started for the back door.

"They're comin'!" Wheeler cried.

Slocum moved toward the horses. He heard rifle shots. He had to get the girl out of there.

"Can you ride, Rebecca?"

She nodded, but when he put her on the pinto, she almost tumbled off.

Slocum grabbed the reins of the stallion. It could carry them double. Wheeler would have to ride the gray or the pinto.

"Wheeler!" Slocum called.

The Sharps went off inside the ranch house.

Slocum put Rebecca on the black and then swung into the saddle behind her.

"Wheeler!" he called again.

But the rancher never made it out.

Slocum heard crashing glass and breaking wood. He drew his pistol.

A rider came around the side of the house.

Slocum shot him in the chest.

He could not wait for Wheeler. He spurred the black toward the north, driving away as hard as the stallion could run. It carried him and the girl without any trouble.

Some of the kid's men gave chase. Slocum outdistanced them on the stallion. He outran the bullets that flew from behind him.

The men dropped off in the dust. Their mounts just couldn't catch the fresh stallion. Slocum rode a couple of extra miles to make sure that he had lost them.

Rebecca Wheeler listed in front of him.

He touched her face. "Which way, honey?"

Rebecca lifted her eyes. "That way."

"You sure?"

She nodded and closed her eyes.

Slocum followed her directions. He hoped that she wasn't too delirious to know where she was going. The wound on Rebecca's arm would not have been a problem for a larger man, but it might kill the girl if he didn't get her settled in a hurry.

When the men broke into his house, Robert Wheeler had cried for Slocum to run. But Slocum had not heard him because he was already in motion. Cooper's men closed in around Wheeler.

The kid was there with a pistol. "Check the house for the girl and the rebel."

Wheeler glared at him. "This won't work. Cooper's grasping at straws. He can't bully me into selling out."

One of the men put a gun in Wheeler's back. "Want me to blow out his guts, Kid?"

Wheeler tensed as the kid hesitated.

"No, let him live. Cooper wants to talk to him before it's all over. We might have to kill him later."

Wheeler waited while they searched the ranch house.

"Find 'em?" the kid asked.

"No."

He frowned. "No? Where are they?"

"The rebel got away with the girl. He was on this stallion. We couldn't rightly catch him."

The kid grimaced. "That's bad. But not all that bad. Cooper needs Wheeler to sign the papers. The girl doesn't mean a thing."

Wheeler smiled. "I wouldn't be so sure about that."

The kid gestured toward the door. "Put him on a horse."

Two men started to lead Wheeler away.

"You'll see!" the rancher cried. "I'll have the last laugh."

"Put a gag on him," the kid said. "Leave him that way until we reach the ranch."

"What about the rebel?" someone asked.

"He's gone. For now," the kid replied. "But he'll turn up sooner or later. He has to, otherwise I won't get a chance to kill him."

* * *

Slocum saw the edge of the forest ahead of him. He guided the stallion along a dry tree line. Some of the trees had wilted in the heat. It could burn easily if a stray spark ignited it.

He looked at the girl. "Rebecca?"

She lifted her eyes. "Just a little bit farther."

Slocum continued along the tree line. He saw the eaves of a cabin in the dried brush. The forest had grown around the place, leaving it almost invisible in the trees.

He carried the girl into the cabin. It was musty inside, but there was a place for her to lie down on a crude bunk.

"Father used to bring me here as a girl," Rebecca said. "There's a well outside. Can you get me some water? I'm so thirsty."

Slocum tried the pump handle behind the cabin. The well had gone dry. He got the canteen from the saddle of the stallion. Rebecca drank and then reclined on a cornshuck mattress.

"How's your wing?" Slocum asked.

"Sore. I just want to close my eyes."

She drifted off to sleep.

Slocum left the canteen beside her. He got up and started for his mount. He knew what he had to do. And he wanted to do it fast.

Evening had fallen over the Cooper Cattle Company. Robert Wheeler's face was partially hidden by shadows. He had been waiting all day to meet with Cooper. Wheeler had a surprise for his captor.

The kid had delivered Wheeler to his boss's office.

Cooper sat behind the desk, glaring at his rival. "You lasted a lot longer'n most, Wheeler. Now all you have to do is sign the Lazy River C over to me. I'll see you get a fair price."

"Ten percent of the true value?"

"More like twenty," Cooper replied. "I figure your place to be worth a thousand. I'll give you two hundred dollars."

Wheeler leaned back in his chair. "All right."

Cooper frowned. "What?"

"I said, all right. I'll sign whatever you want me to. Just show me pen and paper."

"You mean it?" Cooper asked.

Wheeler nodded. "I do."

Cooper spread out the papers on his desk. "Sign there. And there. Yes, you're doing the right thing, Wheeler."

Wheeler inked the agreements and dropped the pen. "Now, let me go. I won't bother you any more."

"Can't do that."

Wheeler laughed. "There's a lot of things you can't do."

Cooper frowned. "What're you getting at?"

"Just wait till you try to claim title on my land," Wheeler replied. "You'll be sorry."

"Why?"

"Because you can't transfer the deed without my daughter. Everything I own is part hers. I fixed it the day she turned twenty-one. That land is half hers. You can't take title without her signature on the papers."

Cooper's eyes grew wide. "You're lying."

"Try to put a claim on the land," Wheeler said. "You'll see. I fixed it all legal."

"But I had that lawyer killed!"

Wheeler scowled at his rival. "So it was you!"

"Yes, it was my men. But you can't prove it. And I think you're lying about this. The lawyer never made it to town."

"I filed those papers last year," Wheeler said.

"You're bluffing."

"Call my hand," Wheeler challenged.

"Jimmy!" Cooper called. "Get him out of here."

The kid appeared to take Wheeler away. "You want me to fix him, boss?"

"No," Cooper replied. "I'll have to study on this. In the meantime, you and the others keep looking for that girl."

"Sure, boss." He started to drag Wheeler out.

"Kid?"

"Yeah, boss?"

Cooper sighed. "Tell the woman to come see me."

The kid smiled. "I'm on it, boss."

He dragged Wheeler out into the hall. "You get to live a little longer, pops."

"I'm glad my daughter got away," Wheeler cried. "She'll sink you all."

The kid pushed him forward. "Shut up."

Cooper leaned back behind his desk. He had to keep Wheeler breathing for a while. When they found the rebel, they would make it look like Slocum had done all of the damage.

Belle appeared in the doorway of his office. "What do you want, Cooper?" she asked.

"Honey, you know exactly what I want. Now get up to that bedroom before I make you pay for your sass."

15

Belle stood next to the bed with her eyes on the floor. She hated Cooper. She was thinking of ways to kill him.

"You're mighty pretty," the rancher said from across the room.

Belle needed something to stab him with. Get him in the eye. The others would punish her, but at least she could do some damage to the man who had killed her gambler.

"I'm not going to hurt you," Cooper said.

"That's big of you," Belle sneered.

Cooper frowned. "There's no need for that kind of talk. I've never been one for hitting women, and I sure don't want you to put me in the mood. Let's have a little smile."

Belle glared at him. "You go to hell, Cooper."

He nodded, smiling. "We can have it that way, too." A knife flashed in his hand. "I can cut the buttons off the front of your dress, or you can unbutton them for me. I'm giving you a choice, Belle."

She tore away the top of her dress. Her breasts were free. Cooper's eyes grew wide.

"I'll only let you do it because you aren't killing me," Belle told him. "But I won't enjoy it one bit."

"I don't care if you do or not, dear." He moved toward her.

Belle drew back against the wall. "What did you do to Tyler?"

"I shipped him back East."

"You killed him!"

He lifted the knife again. "Put your hands away from your chest. Go on, if you know what's good for you."

Belle dropped her hands.

He played with her. His lips rolled around on her skin. It made her flesh crawl, but it was better than dying.

How long would he let her stay alive? When would he be finished with her? How long before she ended up like Jensen?

Cooper drew back from her. "Now, the rest of your dress."

She climbed out of the garment. Her body gleamed in the light of the oil lamp. She put her hands over her breasts again.

"Modest," Cooper chuckled. "Very becoming."

She blushed and looked away. She had been a prostitute before, but Belle figured she really did not deserve a man like Cooper. Fate had paid her back for a lot of bad moves.

"Lie on the bed," Cooper told her.

Belle stretched out on satin sheets. Where the hell had Cooper found satin sheets in the wilds of Oklahoma? He was loco.

"Spread your legs."

She hesitated.

"Do it, woman!"

Belle obeyed him.

"Now play with yourself. Go on—"

He came closer with the lamp.

Belle felt dirty. No man had ever made her feel so low. It was a sorry end to her schemes.

"I won't do it," she said. "To hell with you." She sat up.

Cooper gawked at her. "I want it my way. I pay you for it."

"I almost wish you'd kill me," Belle said. "At least that wouldn't be so humiliating."

Cooper pulled down his pants. "Lie back."

She collapsed on the mattress. "Well, come on you little peckerhead, do it and get it over with."

"I'll make you pay for such insolence." He blew out the lamp.

Cooper climbed on top of her. He prodded her, but his cock was not hard.

"Having trouble?" Belle said with a laugh.

She no longer cared what he did to her. She would defy him all the way. He was a petty little shit with a soft dick. He couldn't hurt her enough to make a difference.

Cooper kept humping her. "I'll show you."

She felt him getting hard. "Maybe you will, after all."

But he never pushed inside her. Cooper's body gave a jolt. He collapsed on top of her.

Somebody lifted the rancher off Belle.

She sat up. "Who's there?"

"It's me, Belle."

"John! You came for me."

Slocum tossed Belle her dress. "Let's get out of here. I got a sick girl needs tending."

"Can we make it?"

"Just get dressed," Slocum replied.

He looked down at Cooper's body. The rancher was still breathing. Slocum hadn't hit him very hard.

"I should plug him right here," Slocum said.

"How did you get in here?" Belle asked.

The tall man shrugged. "Things are lax right now. You seen Wheeler?"

"They got him."

Slocum started for the window. "If you got any medicine, bring it."

"I have some powders and liquids. Who's hurt?"

"The Wheeler girl," Slocum replied.

Belle put her hands on her hips.

Slocum pointed a finger at her. "Don't say it. Just get your stuff, or I'll leave you for the kid."

Belle hurried to her task. In a few minutes, Slocum was lowering her out the window. He came down behind her. The black was waiting for him. He put Belle in the saddle and climbed up behind her.

Slocum walked the black away from the ranch. Nobody saw him. He picked up the pace when they were out on the range. He hoped he could find the cabin again in the dark.

The black held steady against a hot breeze. There was a moon, but dark clouds soon covered it over. They weren't really rain clouds. Just black clumps in the sky. Tornado weather.

"Where are we going?" Belle cried.

"To the woods!"

Belle hung on to the saddle horn. The cowboy had come back to save her. Now, if they could stay away from Cooper, they might have a chance.

"That's real bad lump, Mr. Cooper. The reb really got you."

"Shut up, you idiot!"

The kid backed away, frowning. "I don't like to be called names, Mr. Cooper. You hear me?"

"Hear this! That saddle tramp has come in here and wrecked all of my plans. You've got to stop him once and for all."

The kid smiled. "Okay, but I'm gonna need your help, Mr. Cooper."

"Me?"

"Yeah, it'll take you and the old man to get it done."

"Wheeler?"

"You see what I'm gettin' at, Mr. Cooper?"

Cooper smiled. "I think so. But how did Slocum get in and out of here so easily?"

The kid looked at the floor. "Well, Mr. Cooper, the reb shot us up pretty good today. Some was killed, others wounded. We had some boys up and quit. It's one thing to talk about guns, it's another to face 'em head on."

"How many good men do you have left?"

"Counting me? One."

Cooper waved his hand. "You can hire more men. Until then, I want you to stop that rebel. Find him, and kill him."

The kid sat down in a wooden chair. "Let me study on this, Mr. Cooper. You need the girl. The reb has her. Seems to me like he's the kind of man you could smoke out with a deal. And why not try to pay him off? It'd be the easiest way."

Cooper's eyes narrowed. "Are you afraid to face him?"

The kid laughed. "No. I ain't afraid to face him. That's gonna happen either way. I'm just talkin' about gettin' the girl first."

A smirk appeared on the rancher's face. "You know, Jimmy, I think I can tell you where to find the rebel and the girl. There's this hunting cabin—"

Slocum threw open the door of the cabin. "Rebecca?"

She was still sleeping on the bunk. Slocum knelt beside her. She looked so pale and sickly.

Belle pushed him out of the way. "Let me at her."

He watched her doctor the wound. She also gave Rebecca a potion. The girl immediately broke a sweat on her brow.

Rebecca opened her eyes. "Who—"

"Your guardian angel," Belle replied. "Now close your eyes and go back to sleep."

"How is she?" Slocum asked.

Belle glared at him. "Your little girlfriend is going to be fine. That isn't anything more than a scratch on her arm. I think she was done in by all the excitement."

"We had plenty of that," Slocum said.

"I'll bet you did!"

Slocum grabbed Belle and kissed her. She resisted for a few moments. Then she kissed him back.

"We can't do it in front of the girl," Belle said.

Slocum took her hand. "Outside."

They both wanted it.

Belle lay down on the ground. She lifted her dress and then spread her legs. Slocum knelt down in front of her.

"Do it."

He lay on top of her. Belle guided him in. They only shook for a few minutes before he finished.

Slocum rolled off her. He got up and went into the cabin. He felt Rebecca's forehead. She was cool and dry.

"How's your honey?" Belle asked sarcastically.

"She's alive."

Belle was about to go into a tirade when gunshots erupted from outside the cabin.

Slugs tore through the wood of the door.

Slocum pushed Belle down. He knelt next to Rebecca. His Colt was in his hand.

"Slocum!"

The voice rolled over the woods.

"That you, Kid?" Slocum cried. If he could make him talk, he might get a line on him and get off a shot in his direction.

"We want to deal," the kid said.

Slocum had heard only one gun. He wondered if there were any more hands with the kid. He raised up and fired a few shots out the window.

Slocum ducked down, listening for more gunfire. But the kid did not shoot back. No one did.

"He's alone," Slocum whispered.

"Give us the girl," the kid cried. "Tomorrow, dawn."

"No good," Slocum replied.

The kid laughed. "This ain't between you and me, Slocum. We got to get the girl back to her father. She'll be all right. Mr. Cooper is going to give 'em a fair deal on their ranch."

Rebecca sat up. "Yes," she said. "I'll sell. Anything to be rid of this burden."

Slocum looked into her eyes. "That's no good, Becky. He wants to kill us all. But I have a plan, so you have to trust me."

She nodded. "I do."

"Then don't worry when I say some hateful things. I won't really mean them. But I've got to deal with Cooper. It's the only way to get your father back alive."

She began to cry.

Belle crawled up beside her. She also began to cry. She took Rebecca's frail hand.

Slocum lifted his head. "Kid, this girl doesn't mean a thing to me, but I know she means a lot to Cooper. I want money. Hard, cold currency."

"We can do it," the kid called back. "Give her up to me now."

"No," Slocum replied. "I want the money first."

"I can come in after you!" the kid cried.

Slocum scoffed. "You knew where I was and you only came by yourself, Kid. You're alone. It's between you and me, now. But there's no reason to hurt the Wheelers. Have the old man sign off the ranch. Then it won't matter."

Rebecca raised up again. "He can't do that without me. I have to sign the papers, too."

"That's why he wants you," Slocum said. "We can trick him."

Rebecca nodded. "Get my father back. Please."

Belle looked at Slocum. "You can work this good. Turn it around on Cooper. He'll probably try to double-cross you, anyway."

Slocum had to think on it. "Go back to Cooper, Kid. Tell him I want a thousand dollars. In gold."

"Now you're talkin'!" the kid cried.

Slocum heard a horse pounding away a few moments later. Dust stirred through the forest. The wind picked up like it was following the path of the Cimarron Kid.

He looked at Belle. "You got any notions about this?"

She began to ponder.

"I don't want to hurt the girl or her daddy."

Belle glanced sideways at him. "When did you turn so pure of heart?"

"The Yankees killed most of me, honey, but they didn't kill it all. A child like that—"

"She's no child."

Slocum shook his head. "Jealous. You don't understand. What I feel for that girl doesn't have anything to do with what's between my legs. I save that for you."

Belle raised an eyebrow. "You want to?"

"I think I could."

She reached into her bag. "Here, I got some whiskey. Let's both have a snort before we do."

They drained the rest of the bottle in two swigs. Slocum felt the warmth spreading over him. Belle also seemed to relax.

"Let's go outside again," she told him.

Slocum was ready.

"Like mare and stallion," Belle said. She went down on all fours.

Slocum penetrated her from behind.

Their bodies shook until he shot again.

Slocum stood up when he was finished.

Belle frowned at him. "Just have your fun and go!"

Slocum went inside, kneeling beside the girl's bed.

Belle came in behind him. "Are you ready to listen to me, cowboy?"

"Say your piece, woman, but make it quick. I don't want the angels comin' for this precious creature."

"Spare me," Belle replied. "I don't care about your girl-friend. But this is what you have to do—"

16

"He's ready to deal, Mr. Cooper."

The rancher looked up at the Cimarron Kid. "Then the rebel was at the cabin?"

"Yes, sir. I think he's got the girl with him. I'm pretty sure of it."

Cooper poured his glass full of whiskey. He drank it down. His eyes were glassy and his speech was a little slurred.

"How are we gonna do it?" the kid asked.

Cooper shook his head. "I'm not sure. I've seen to it that you'll have some help. Some men will be arriving by Friday. They're coming up from Texas to help you finish the job."

The kid bristled. "I can handle it, Cooper."

"You haven't been able to get the job done so far," Cooper replied.

The kid's eyes grew narrow. He grabbed the bottle of red-eye from Cooper's desk. After he had knocked back a healthy snort, he slammed the bottle in front of the rancher.

"One day you're gonna wish you hadn't talked to me like that, Cooper. You hear me?"

The rancher waved him off. "You're too touchy, Kid. I didn't mean anything. Don't lose your head."

The kid deflated a little. He sat in a wooden chair. He wanted the tall rebel in his sights. Killing Slocum would vindicate him.

"Keep the rebel on a string," Cooper said. "When the guns get here, you know what to do."

"Yes, sir."

"Don't kill the girl, not yet. I need her. If the old man is telling the truth about his land being in both names, she'll have to sign the deed over to me."

"Then what?" the kid asked.

"Take her," Cooper replied. "You've had your eye on her. Use her. But when you throw her away, make it look good. As far as you know, the girl and her father packed up and moved back East."

"No trace," the kid replied.

He wondered if he could kill a woman. A pretty woman with a sweet nature. He frowned. He saw the rebel in his sights, but not Rebecca Wheeler.

"Something wrong, Jimmy?"

"No, Mr. Cooper. I was just studyin' on it. That rebel ain't gonna be easy to take. But I'm sure I can do it."

Cooper pointed to the door of his office. "You've done your duty, Kid. Why don't you have some supper and get some sleep?"

"I've got to go back out to see the rebel."

"In the morning," Cooper replied. "Let him sweat."

"He might run."

Cooper shook his head. "Slocum wants to get something out of this. What's the girl to him? If he's ready to deal, then we have no problem."

The kid left his boss. He wasn't so sure about Slocum. He figured the tall son of Dixie had it for the woman. Maybe the kid had it, too. He tried not to think about having to shoot Rebecca. But there it was, the thorn in his heart.

"Damn."

He walked out into the yard. The place was quiet. The bunkhouse was almost empty expect for two wounded men.

"How ya doin', Kid?"

"You back already, Cimarron?"

The kid ignored them. He climbed into his own bunk, staring up at the ceiling. Sweat broke out on his face. Suddenly the kid named Jimmy did not feel like killing anyone. What had taken the starch out of him?

Rebecca Wheeler.

Jimmy sat up on the bed. "No, not her."

His heart was pounding. He had been rough and rude with the Wheeler girl, but it had all been an act. He suddenly felt remorse for shooting the girl's father. A tear trickled out of his eye.

The kid wiped it away. He hadn't been ready for what had happened inside him. He loved Rebecca Wheeler. And it made him think crazy thoughts.

He leaned back on the cot. He couldn't go against Cooper, but he wouldn't be able to kill the Wheelers, even though he knew Cooper would demand it.

His eyes focused on the ceiling. He said her name. He said it again. Why was he feeling like this? It had never happened to him before. He kept seeing her face. Then he would wince when he imagined the revolver going off. It twisted inside him like the spring of a clock. He actually felt a pain in his chest.

He closed his eyes, trying to sleep, but the pain would not go away, and he started to cry again.

Slocum sat by Rebecca Wheeler, holding her soft hand. She was sleeping soundly on the cot. Some of the color had returned to her face. Slocum knew he had to find her something to eat, but he just sat there a few more minutes, admiring her face.

He wasn't sure about the plan Belle had laid out. It made sense most of the time, but there was always that little moment of doubt. There were ways to make sure. Slocum planned to use them.

Belle sat up behind him. "John?"

She got up off the floor where she had been sleeping. There were coals burning in the fireplace, the embers left from a fire Slocum had started. Belle threw some dry twigs on the coals. The twigs burst into flames.

"Careful," Slocum warned. "We don't want too many sparks going up that chimney. Those woods could go up in a hurry."

Belle scowled at him. "You let the fire go out in the first place."

Slocum decided to ignore her. Belle was just grouchy because he was sitting with Rebecca. A woman couldn't stand to see a man she liked being nice to another woman.

"Is she still alive?" Belle asked.

"She's fine," Slocum replied.

Belle looked out the window. "I wonder if I could shoot something in these woods."

"You?"

"Hey, I was raised on a farm in Illinois. I can shoot."

Slocum gestured to the rifle. "It's awful dark out there, but go ahead. See what you can scare up."

Belle struck an indignant pose. "You don't think I could."

"No, I don't."

She grabbed the rifle and went out of the cabin.

Slocum shook his head. He wondered if she would shoot herself. He didn't need a second patient to tend.

Rebecca stirred on the cot. She opened her eyes. When she saw Slocum, she pulled her hand away and tried to sit up.

"Easy, girl."

"My father!" she said. "Is he—"

"He's still alive," Slocum replied.

Rebecca put a hand on her chest. "Thank God. I was dreaming that someone had killed him."

Slocum lifted the canteen to her lips. "Have a drink of water, Becky. You're doin' fine. How's the arm feel?"

Rebecca looked at the bandage. "Not as bad as it was. I feel like myself. Except that I'm groggy. And I—"

Rebecca froze when the shot went off.

Slocum turned toward the back door. "Well, she did it."

"Who?"

Slocum looked at the girl. "Belle. Don't worry, she's just trying to get my goat."

Rebecca leaned back on the cot again. "Perhaps I should rest some more."

"That's best."

She did not close her eyes. Instead she glared sideways at Slocum. Her gaze made him feel weak inside.

"I remember things," Rebecca said. "You promised the kid you'd give me up for a thousand dollars."

"That's all part of the plan," Slocum replied. "Don't worry, I won't give you to him. Not if everything goes right."

"The kid also called you Slocum. Is that your real name?"

He nodded. "As close as it gets."

"I misjudged you," she told him. "I thought you were a good man. But you're really a bald-faced liar."

He lowered his eyes. "I probably am."

The back door flew open. Belle came in holding something in her hand. She had a hen turkey by the neck.

"There," she said to Slocum. "Caught it feeding out back. There's a late moon tonight."

She threw the bird at Slocum's feet.

"What you want me to do?" he asked.

"I shot it; you clean it," Belle replied.

Slocum hadn't plucked a turkey in a while, but he found the task to be just as revolting as he always had. Still, he did it for the girl. She needed to eat, to regain her strength. He also gutted the bird.

Belle watched him from the door. "Wish we had some more water. That canteen is about empty."

He handed her the cleaned turkey. "Get this on the fire. I'll see if I can prime the pump."

He used the rest of the water from the canteen to prime the well. It worked. The water was murky, but it was wet. He washed the turkey blood from his hands and then filled the canteen.

Belle had the turkey over the coals when he went back inside.

"You get the well working?" she asked.

He nodded. "The water's a little muddy."

"We can strain it through cloth."

He looked at the fire. "How long till we eat?"

"Hours. Not till after daybreak."

"I'm gonna sleep," Slocum replied. "Don't make too much racket."

He stretched out on the floor. Sleep came easily. He rested until the kid called for him at dawn.

"Slocum?"

The tall man opened his green eyes.

"I'm back, Slocum! Are you in there?"

Slocum saw the purple glow outside the cabin. He reached for his Colt. Belle was right there beside him.

"Slocum?" the kid called again. "You better answer, or I'm gonna start shootin'!"

"I'm here," Slocum called back. "Don't come any closer or you'll be dodging bullets."

"I came to talk," the kid replied. "Just like we said."

Rebecca sat up on her cot. "Don't let him get me."

"Nobody's gonna hurt you," Slocum told her.

Belle leaned closer to the tall man. "Forget about her, John. Set it up with the kid, the way we planned it."

He nodded. "Okay, but this better work."

"It will," Belle insisted. "It will."

"How's Miss Rebecca?" the kid asked.

"Never mind," Slocum called back. "Here's my terms. You come back here tomorrow and bring the money."

"Not tomorrow. It's gonna take Cooper a while to raise that kind of money. We're comin' on Sunday. Take it or leave it."

Slocum frowned. "Sunday? He's bringing more men."

"It won't matter," Belle replied. "Sunday's better, anyway."

"How 'bout it, Slocum?"

"Sunday'll do," the tall man replied. "Daybreak. If you aren't here by then, I'll take the girl and leave."

"We'll be here," the kid replied.

Slocum nodded. "I knew it. More men. Cooper's bringing them in, probably from Texas."

He heard the kid riding off again.

"It won't matter," Belle insisted. "Not if we do it like I say."

Slocum looked at the girl. "I guess your way is best. It makes the most sense. We could leave now, but we won't have Mr. Wheeler."

Belle looked into the fire. "You know, I saw him once. He's not a bad looking man. If he—"

Slocum jabbed her. "Watch your mouth. The girl."

"Sorry."

Slocum sat beside Rebecca again.

She was sleeping soundly. She was still weak, but at least she had become more coherent. That meant she was getting better.

"This bird'll be ready soon."

He took Rebecca's hand.

"I haven't ever had turkey for breakfast," Belle went on. "I hope there's some white meat on this scrawny thing."

Slocum gently shook Rebecca. "Honey, you want to eat?"

But the girl did not wake up. She only lay there, looking like an angel.

Slocum wasn't going to let anyone hurt her. Not even if it meant risking his life.

The kid rode back toward the Cooper spread. He coughed in the dust. A hot wind began to blow from the south. It was going to be another day of killer heat.

Things had gone well with Slocum, the kid thought. The rebel had taken the bait. He was greedy, like all men.

The kid flinched. He kept thinking about the two mistakes he had made. He had asked about the woman, which let Slocum know that there was a weakness inside him. And he had said *we* would be back. *We.* Was Slocum smart enough to figure out that he would be bringing back some help?

What if Slocum ran?

No, he wouldn't give up the money. The rebel needed a stake. He was dead broke from working for the Wheelers after Rebecca had bailed him out of jail.

Jimmy shivered when he thought about the girl. Maybe he would marry her. That might keep Cooper quiet.

The rancher wanted blood. He wouldn't rest until Wheeler was dead. And after the father was gone, Cooper wouldn't let the daughter live to bear witness against him.

"I ain't killin' the girl," he said out loud.

Cooper was waiting for the kid when he got back. The rancher sat on the porch with a shotgun across his lap. He nursed a whiskey bottle.

"Well, Jimmy?"

"He's ready. Sunday mornin'. It's all set."

Cooper smiled and sighed. "It will be over. The Lazy River C will be mine. And the Wheelers will be dead."

The kid replied, "Yes, sir."

But Jimmy knew that it might not happen that way in the final reckoning.

17

Slocum stared out the cabin window, peering into the darkness. It was Saturday night, the evening before the switch was supposed to take place. Slocum still had his doubts, but he was going to try to stack the deck in his favor before it all happened.

"Do you think he might come tonight?" Rebecca asked.

He looked back at the girl. She was sitting on the edge of the bed. She had gotten stronger with Belle's care.

"He'll wait till tomorrow," Slocum replied. "But don't fret. You won't be here when he comes."

Belle came up behind him, peering over his shoulder. "I don't see anything. Maybe they just gave up."

Slocum got up and moved over to sit by Rebecca. "Honey, you feel like you can ride?"

Rebecca nodded. "But I'm afraid."

"You should be," Belle chimed in.

Slocum brushed her off with a dirty look.

Belle kept looking out of the window. "Nobody yet."

Slocum took Rebecca's hand. "I got to leave now."

"No—"

"Belle's goin' with me," Slocum went on. "You have to be alone for a while. But nobody's gonna hurt you."

"Why do I have to go?" Belle asked.

"You're gonna need the horse," he told her. "You can't stay here, not with the kid on the way. And if I'm gonna try to save Wheeler, you can't come along to drag me down."

Belle gave in to the demands of logic.

Slocum tried to smile at Rebecca, but he wasn't very good at it.

"Are you really going after my father?" she asked.

He nodded. "I'm gonna try. Belle there figured it. It's not a bad plan. I hope it'll work."

Rebecca lowered her eyes. "I'm sorry that I called you a liar."

"You were right all along, honey."

She started to cry. Slocum got up. It hurt him to see her sad.

"Little Miss Waterwheel," Belle quipped.

Slocum grabbed her arm. "Come on, Belle. We have to go."

Belle winked at Rebecca. "Don't wait up, sweetie."

Slocum pulled her outside. "I liked it better when you were putting on that fine lady act."

"To hell with you," Belle snapped.

Slocum climbed into the saddle of the black stallion. "Come on." He held out his hand to her.

Belle folded her arms over her chest. "I'm not going."

Slocum sighed. "Suit yourself. I'd hate to see what will happen when Cooper gets hold of you again."

"All right. Give me a hand."

She sat in front of him on the saddle of the stallion. "Ever done it on a horse, John?"

"Shut up, Belle. Just shut up."

He spurred the black and headed straight for the Cooper Cattle Company.

Slocum reined back on the stallion. "There it is."

Belle saw the lights below them. "Where are we?"

"On a ridge above Cooper's place," Slocum replied. "Get down and put an ear to the wind."

They both dismounted.

Slocum stood on the ridge, gazing down at the ranch. "He's having a party," the tall man said. "He thinks it's all over tomorrow."

Belle put her hand on his shoulder. "I'm starting to be afraid, John. I don't know if it will work."

"Just take the stallion," Slocum replied. "Go where we said. Wait for me. I should be there before noon."

"John—"

"Whining won't help, woman. Now, go."

She pressed her body against his. "We haven't done it in a couple of days. Can we do it one more time?"

"Here?"

Belle knelt down on all fours in the dirt. "Like horses."

Slocum felt the need. It had come on him unexpectedly. He dropped behind her and humped her hard.

When they were finished, he stood up again and looked toward the festive ranch house.

Belle jumped to her feet. "I swear, you have no manners, John."

"Just get back and take the girl away from that cabin. Wait for me like I said."

Belle mounted the stallion. "I hope you make it, John. I really do. But if you don't, look me up in hell."

She turned the stallion and vanished into the night.

Slocum kept his eyes on the ranch house. Music lilted over the dry plain. There was dancing. Corn liquor was probably flowing.

The tall man felt lonely all of a sudden. He wished that Rebecca was there. He wanted to dance with her. He bet she was the kind of girl who liked to dance up a storm.

The wind picked up a little. He could no longer hear the music. The celebration went on for a long time before the lights went out. The men would be hung over. They'd never be able to guess what Slocum had in mind.

He wondered how many guns Cooper had purchased. He hated the man for his arrogance. Maybe Wheeler could go to the marshal and sink Cooper.

The last light went out in the ranch house. It was probably close to midnight. Cooper's men had to ride at dawn. Their heads would still be thick from corn whiskey.

Slocum lay down on the ground. He tried to close his eyes. Dust whipped over his face in the wind. He had to pull up his bandanna to keep the grit from sanding his face.

He found he couldn't sleep, so he sat up again, peering toward the dark outline of the Cooper place. He had about five hours until daylight.

Slocum braced himself against the gritty breeze, listening for the far, lonely cry of a rooster.

The Mexican girl pressed her body against the Cimarron Kid. Her hands came up to his face. She pulled him down for a long kiss.

"You taste like onion," he told her.

The girl started to slap him. Jimmy caught her with his gun hand. He twisted her wrist until she went down on one knee.

"Get out of my sight." He let go of her wrist.

"You don' wan' me?" she asked.

"No, not tonight."

Usually, her body was enough for the kid. But he was thinking about someone else. Rebecca Wheeler kept drifting through his mind. What was it about her face?

The kid had never felt anything so painful. He lay back on the cot. He flexed his gun hand. It was ready.

He sat up again. They would take the rebel in the morning. Then the kid would have to decide what to do with the woman. He couldn't kill her. Not for any amount of money. Cooper would just have to understand.

He tried to lie down again. Cooper had brought in a half-dozen guns from Texas. What if he turned them on the kid? Cooper hadn't exactly been pleased with Jimmy's performance. The kid had made a few mistakes.

Reaching for the holster on the bedpost, he checked his pistol again. There wouldn't be too much gunplay, not if the rebel was smart. What if Rebecca got hit with a stray shot? At that thought, the kid let out a cry that should have come from a wounded animal.

"Rebecca." He whispered her name over and over.

Someone moved toward him in the shadows.

Jimmy raised his gun at the Mexican girl.

"I come back," she said.

He waved the weapon. *"Vamos. Pronto."*

She left again, moving out of the bunkhouse.

The Cimarron Kid lay back and waited for the dawn.

Slocum opened his eyes when he heard the sound of horses passing by over the rustle of the morning wind. He had been dozing. His green eyes focused on the seven riders who headed for the cabin in the woods.

The kid led the way. They were riding fast in the predawn. Slocum hoped that Belle had done her job. If she had taken the girl away, then there wouldn't be any problem.

Slocum waited until the riders were out of sight. He checked his pistol. It was a quiet Sunday morning on the ranch. Everyone would be sleeping. Slocum could slip in and out before anyone knew it.

He started down the incline.

The shadows around the place were still long and dark. Clouds rolled down from the west, covering the sky. Maybe they were rain clouds. The drought didn't seem like much of a problem compared to the task of rescuing Wheeler.

When he was halfway to the ranch house, Slocum knelt down and studied the structures. There didn't seem to be any sentries on the roof. Cooper had probably sent all his men with the kid, to make sure he didn't mess up the deal.

Belle had come up with another plan. While the kid was riding to the cabin, Slocum could sneak in and get the father. Then they could meet again at the Wheeler place. Wheeler and Rebecca had to get the marshal while they were still alive.

Slocum began to move again.

He heard a horse snorting. He knelt, but it was only an echo from the stable. The tall man started forward in the wind. The clouds seemed to hang low over the ground. Grit pelted him in the hot air.

Slocum ran over the empty barnyard, making for the ranch house. He figured Wheeler was somewhere inside. Slocum aimed to free him.

The kid stood at the edge of the woods, looking at the cabin between the trees. "Slocum!"

No reply came from the cabin.

"Slocum, you can bring the girl out. I've got the money."

They had their rifles ready. As soon as the girl was in their grasp, Slocum was to be laced by everyone. They'd take no chances in leaving him alive. They were going to cheat the kid out of a showdown with the rebel.

"I ain't kiddin' around, Slocum," the kid called. "I've got six men with me. You don't want us to hurt you."

The wind rustled the dry leaves.

"We could burn him out," one of the hired guns suggested.

"No. We have to get the girl alive," the kid said. "And nobody touches her. You got that?"

The gunman pointed at the cabin. "Want us to go in?"

The kid squinted into the shadows. "Slocum!"

"It's awful windy. Maybe he can't hear us."

Jimmy nodded toward the cabin. "Go on. But remember, Cooper has to have the girl alive."

The hired guns moved to do their job. Jimmy stayed on the edge of the woods, waiting for them. He didn't want Rebecca to know he was one of the desperate sort that Cooper had signed on.

They trickled back out of the woods. "Nobody in there, Kid."

"Damn! He—" The kid peered in the direction of the Cooper place.

"What's wrong, Kid?"

"Come on," Jimmy replied. "We've got to get back to the ranch. I think I just made another mistake, and it's a whopper."

Slocum slipped around behind the ranch house. He listened for a moment in the shadows. He heard snoring from a back room. Was it Wheeler?

His fingers gripped the butt of the Colt. If he let off a shot, it would alert everyone to his presence. Cooper might have other men stashed in the bunkhouse.

He stepped up onto the back porch. The door was open. Slocum slipped through the kitchen, moving toward a narrow corridor.

The snoring echoed through the hall.

Slocum moved slowly, stopping at a closed door to listen.

The snoring was coming from the room. Slocum opened the door. He saw Wheeler lying on a sofa, with his hands and feet tied.

He roused Wheeler from an uncomfortable sleep. The rancher's eyes grew wide. He tried to talk. Slocum put a finger to his lips.

Wheeler nodded.

"Rebecca is safe," the tall man whispered. "I'm gonna try to get you out of here."

He untied Wheeler. The rancher tried to stand, but his legs were sore and stiff. Slocum told him to rub the aching, cramped muscles. Wheeler began to massage his legs.

Slocum stepped to the door. The house was still quiet. Nobody had heard him enter. He looked at Wheeler, who was now standing.

Wheeler took a couple of steps. He was ready. He moved behind Slocum, trying to tiptoe.

Slocum slid out into the hall.

There was a sudden thump in the kitchen.

Slocum pressed his back against the wall. Someone was moving around. Footsteps disappeared into another part of the house.

Wheeler stuck his head into the hall.

Slocum waved for him to come along.

They started toward the kitchen. Slocum held his breath. They had to get to the horses. And they had to hurry. As soon as the kid discovered that they had abandoned the cabin, he would fly back to the ranch with his gunmen.

Slocum hesitated by the archway that led into the kitchen. He peeked around the corner. The kitchen was empty.

The tall man started for the back door. Wheeler followed him through the kitchen. They were almost out when they heard the clicking noise.

"Not one step more!"

Slocum froze, trying to look over his shoulder.

Wheeler also peered into the morning shadows.

Cooper came at them with a double-barreled scattergun.

"What's this? Two rats in the kitchen."

Slocum began to lower his hands.

"Where's the girl, Slocum?" Cooper asked.

But Slocum did not answer him.

And Cooper certainly wasn't ready for what happened next.

18

The wind caught the back door, tearing it away from Slocum's grip. Dust swirled inside the house. Cooper screamed and started to grab his eyes. The shotgun pointed downward.

Slocum grabbed Wheeler and threw him back into Cooper. The rancher fell against the wall. Wheeler bounced off him and then fell to the floor.

The shotgun went off, blowing a hole in the floor.

Slocum drew his Colt. He wanted to end it once and for all. The Colt erupted. Cooper grabbed his chest. Blood poured between the rancher's stubby fingers.

"I'm hit," Cooper moaned.

Wheeler was on his feet, gaping at the wounded man. "He's hit, Slocum. You shot him."

Cooper groaned and leaned forward, gasping. Blood poured from his mouth. His eyes were open, frozen like winter glass.

"He's dead!" Wheeler cried.

"We will be, too, if we don't get the hell out of here. Come on, Wheeler. Those shots'll have everybody awake." He dragged Wheeler away from Cooper.

Slocum knew the sheriff would try to hang him for shooting Cooper, but the sheriff still had to catch him. As soon as he delivered Wheeler to his daughter, Slocum was going to ride on.

They ran across the yard to the stable. A man appeared with a rifle. Slocum shot him in the head. The man tumbled to the ground, twitching.

"Too much killing," Wheeler said.

"There'll be more."

They found a couple of mounts already saddled. Cooper had probably planned to ride to town and register the land deal as soon as the Wheelers signed their ranch over to him.

They mounted up and started away from the ranch.

A lone rifle barked from a rooftop, but their mounts quickly took them out of range.

"Where we going?" Wheeler cried.

"Your place."

If everything had gone according to the plan, the women would be waiting for them at the Lazy River C. Slocum was going to reunite the father and daughter, but the Wheelers would have to find the marshal on their own.

They rode into the stiff wind, trying to see through the drifts of dust. Slocum pulled up his bandanna. Wheeler wrapped his coat around his face. They had to get to the women before the kid figured out what had happened.

The Cimarron Kid rode at an angle to the wind. He was almost to the ranch house when he saw the riders from the east. There were eight of them. The kid turned and dug for the others.

He met the sheriff and seven of his deputies.

"You got trouble?" the sheriff asked.

The kid nodded. "The rebel."

"I shoulda run him out of town."

The sheriff pointed toward the house. He wanted to get out of the wind. It took them a while to find Cooper's body.

"This is bad," the sheriff said.

The kid looked at him. "How?"

"Cooper's dead."

"Shit. That means more for me and you."

The sheriff rubbed his chin. "I could fix it. I got a lawyer friend. It could be ours."

The kid imagined Rebecca Wheeler by his side. "Let's do it, Peters. Take it all. Cash in."

"Gonna be tricky," the sheriff said.

"We'll put our men together. You have that lawyer draw

up a phony will. Cooper will leave this ranch to me."

"And me!" the sheriff insisted.

"We still got to catch the rebel," the kid said.

"And the girl," Peters reminded him. "Let's not forget about her."

"Come on," the kid said. "I know where Cooper keeps his strongbox."

"We got to get after the rebel, Kid."

"As soon as we fill our pockets, Sheriff."

Jimmy would have it all. Wealth. Rebecca at his side. It was better with Cooper gone. It left him more room to move.

Now all he had to do was kill Slocum.

Slocum glanced back over his shoulder. "Dust storm!" he cried to Wheeler. "It's almost on us."

The sky was alive with a dark, sinister vapor. Black swirls roared over them, threatening to leave them gagging on dirt. Slocum spurred his mount. Wheeler came after him. Their only chance was to outrun the storm.

The animals ran their hearts out from fear of the monster behind them. Slocum could see a lump ahead. Sheets of dust had begun to roll across the plain like a shower of grit.

Somehow their horses got through it. Wheeler's ranch house loomed out of the storm. Slocum jumped from the saddle. Wheeler's mount threw him to the ground.

Slocum bent to help him up. Wheeler was able to walk. They stumbled toward the front porch. The door flew open.

Rebecca came out to help her father. She ushered him inside. Slocum came behind them and closed the door.

Sand pelted all sides of the house. The turbulence shook the walls and the roof.

Slocum glanced upward, hoping that the wind didn't tear the rafters off the ranch house.

Rebecca embraced her father. "You're alive. Thank God."

Wheeler frowned at his daughter. "What happened to your arm?"

"I was wounded, remember? John saved me."

Wheeler glanced at Slocum. "John fixed a good many things."

Slocum frowned at them. "Don't get sentimental on me. Even if we get through this dust storm, we still won't be out of trouble."

The house vibrated against the gusts of wind. A window shattered. Dust swirled through the holes that had been used for rifle ports.

"Get the windows covered," Slocum ordered. "Use whatever you can find."

They steeled the windows against the ravages of the gritty wind. There was nothing else to do but wait it out. The storm whirled around them, shaking the house to its very foundation.

"I hope that roof doesn't go!" Slocum cried.

"Look at this," the kid said.

He pointed out the window. The sheriff could also see the dust storm that moved over the plain. Cooper's house was on the edge of the storm. The windows rattled, but the house was in no real danger.

"That's headin' straight for the Wheeler place."

The sheriff frowned. "So?"

The kid shook his head. "What'd you do before you became a lawman?"

"I was a bounty hunter."

"Figgers. Look here, Peters. Wheeler and the rebel ran. Where you think they was runnin' to?"

"Who can say?"

"He went home," the kid said. "Him and the reb headed for Wheeler's place. I bet they're there now."

"Maybe."

The kid sighed. "I'll go check after that storm blows through."

"Hope there's no tornadoes," the sheriff said.

The Cimarron Kid sat down in the chair behind Cooper's desk. He poured some whiskey and lit a cigar. Leaning back in the chair, he propped his boots on the desk.

"Yep, it's gonna be real good, Peters. You just wait and see. When this storm is by us, that rebel is as good as dead."

• • •

Belle walked into the main parlor. "What's going on? I woke from my nap. The house is shaking."

"Dust storm," Slocum said.

She ran to kneel beside him. He put his hand on her shoulder. She looked scared and lonely.

Rebecca sat next to her father. She was quiet. Her eyes were almost closed.

Wheeler looked up at the rafters. "I built this house myself. It'll stand up to a dust storm."

Rebecca fell asleep beside him.

Slocum listened as the wind continued to howl. How could the girl sleep through such a din?

"How long is this going to last?" Belle said.

Slocum sighed. "Too long. It's keeping us from getting the Wheelers out of here."

"I want to leave, too," Belle replied.

"We all need to get out of here," Slocum said. "You've got to get to the marshal, Wheeler."

The rancher shook his head. "I'm not going anywhere."

"But you have to run," Belle chimed in. "Cooper wants to kill you so he can have the Lazy River C for himself."

"This is my home," Wheeler replied. "I won't leave. No one is going to drive me away."

"You've got to see the marshal," Slocum insisted.

"No. Besides, you killed Cooper, John."

Belle gaped at Slocum. "What?"

The tall man shrugged. "It was the best way to end it."

"Well, you were wrong!" Belle cried. "You just got things started. The kid and that sheriff are going to come after you. They're greedier than Cooper was."

"I won't leave," the rancher insisted. "I won't give in again. If I have to die defending my home, I—"

Rebecca raised her head. "Father's right. Will you stay and help us fight, Mr. Slocum?"

The tall man gazed upward. "I don't know if we're going to live that long."

The storm raged all around them. A tremor went through the house.

• • •

The kid stood up behind Cooper's desk. "It's good enough to ride. The wind has died a little."

Sheriff Peters was picking his teeth. "I don't think the rebel woulda run to Wheeler's. I think they went back to that hunting cabin where you found 'em the first time."

"Suit yourself, Sheriff. If you catch him before I do, save the rebel for me. I want to take him in a fair fight."

"Kind of a stupid request, Kid."

"Just do it, lawman."

The kid ran out of the house. He mounted a sorrel in the stable. It was the same animal that he had stolen from Slocum in Elkhart. The wind was still blowing when he rode out.

Peters had not yet assembled his men. That gave the kid a head start on finding the rebel.

As the wind died a little, things began to relax in the ranch house. The rafters no longer shook. Wheeler felt that the occasion called for a shot of good bourbon. He also wanted a cigar.

Rebecca got up and lit a lamp. She went into the kitchen to find something to eat. Belle followed Rebecca to assist her.

Wheeler lit another lamp before he poured the drinks.

"Isn't even noon," he said. "The dust makes it look like nightfall."

"The storm is almost past," Slocum replied. "You and Rebecca must get to Oklahoma City."

Wheeler shook his head. "I told you, I'm staying. Let fate deal my hand, but I'm not going to be afraid of anyone."

He toasted the passing storm.

Slocum sipped his drink. He also rolled a cigarette. The whiskey and the smoke relaxed him a little.

"I rescued you," he told Wheeler. "But you've got to help yourself from here on out. I thought you had more love for that girl than to get her killed."

Wheeler glared at him. "That's enough out of you."

Slocum got up and went into the kitchen. "Becky, you've got to talk your father into leaving."

The girl snapped at Slocum. "Call me Miss Wheeler!"

"I killed Cooper," he told her. "But you've got clear out, in case that sheriff comes after you. He might throw in with the kid."

"My father has made his decision," Rebecca replied curtly. "Now, please leave me alone so I can make dinner." She pushed past him.

He looked at Belle. "Talk to her."

Belle took his arm. "Come out on the porch for a minute."

She guided Slocum outside. The wind had almost stopped. There was still a lot of dust in the air.

"If they stay, it's over for them," Slocum told Belle.

"Forget them, John. You've got to run. Go get the marshal."

Slocum frowned. "Me?"

"You can find him. I know you can. Send him back here. Maybe he can straighten it out."

"What about the Wheelers? Are you saying that you think they should stay here?"

Belle shook her head. "No! But they have to settle down. They're loco right now. Can't you see the way they're acting? Like nothing happened. When they calm down a little, I'll try to get them to leave."

He squinted at her. "When did you become the good Samaritan?"

"I'm doing this for myself, so I can get out of here alive."

"I need a mount," Slocum said.

"The black is still in the barn. Now, go." She kissed him on the lips.

Slocum kissed her back.

Belle pushed him toward the barn.

Slocum ran through the swirling dust. The barn door had been closed, so the stallion was in good shape. Slocum reached for the saddle on the stall door.

A revolver cylinder clicked.

Slocum felt cold iron on his neck.

"Don't move, Reb."

Slocum lifted his hands. "Hello, Kid. It's about time you showed up."

19

The Cimarron Kid had a baffled expression on his face. "What're you talkin' about, Slocum?"

"Come on inside, and I'll tell you."

The kid kept the iron on his neck. "What makes you think I want to listen? You ain't got nothin' to say to me."

Slocum turned to face him. The weapon did not go off. He looked the kid in the eye.

"Come on, Jimmy. Rebecca's inside."

The kid's face went slack. His gun hand trembled slightly. Sweat beaded on his lip.

"What?"

"Rebecca. She's inside, Jimmy. Waitin' for you."

Slocum had him. The kid had called for the girl before. He was sweet on Rebecca. Slocum had to use it until he got an opening.

"Rebecca," the kid said.

"Yeah, she's missed you something fierce."

Jimmy raised the barrel of his pistol. "You better stop funnin' me, Reb. I ain't of a mind to—"

"Suit yourself. If you don't want to see her—"

Jimmy waved toward the house with his weapon. "Get goin', Slocum."

They trudged across the dusty barnyard. The kid kept the gun in Slocum's back. Slocum knew he had to be patient, wait for the right moment.

"Don't try nothin', Reb. I'll kill you, if you do."

They stepped into the kitchen. Belle was not there. Rebecca had also disappeared.

The kid pushed Slocum out into the main parlor.

Wheeler startled as they came in. "Where did he come from?"

"I knew you'd run here," the kid said. "The sheriff didn't believe me. He went to your cabin."

Wheeler shook his head. "You were right, John. I should have run."

Slocum looked at the kid. "We all should have."

"What's that supposed to mean?" the kid asked.

"You know what the sheriff is gonna do to the Wheelers," Slocum replied.

Jimmy frowned. "Now that Cooper's gone, he can let them live. At least the girl."

Slocum chortled derisively. "No, he can't. They know he was part of the conspiracy with Cooper. They hang men who conspire, at least in this territory."

Sweat poured off the kid. "I got to think about this."

"What's to think about?" Slocum said quickly. "If you don't throw in with us, you have to watch Rebecca die."

"No!"

Rebecca moved out of the shadows. "Hello, Jimmy." She smiled.

The kid looked at her for a moment. Then he glanced back at Slocum. The tall man hadn't moved.

"Nice try, Reb."

Slocum nodded toward Rebecca. "You can't kill her, Jimmy."

Rebecca stared straight at the kid. "We mean you no harm, Mr. Cimarron. If you'd like to stay, you can put down your gun and join us for dinner."

The kid shook his head. "I can't stand this."

"You can't kill her," Slocum persisted. "You can't even kill me, now. You wouldn't want Rebecca to see you do it."

"Go ahead," Rebecca said to the kid. "Shoot me, Mr. Cimarron. Then kill my father. But please, shoot me first. I wouldn't want to watch him die."

"Shut up!" Jimmy cried. "Stop it, both of you."

"It's your choice," Rebecca went on. "If you—"

The kid laughed hysterically. "I don't have no choice. I'm in this deep. I've done wrong."

Rebecca moved closer to the kid, putting her hand on his forearm. "Many men do wrong, Mr. Cimarron. But they may repent. They can choose the path of righteousness."

Jimmy looked into her eyes. "You're so beautiful, Miss Rebecca. I'm plumb sorry I shot your paw."

Rebecca smiled. "Give me the gun. Please."

Jimmy handed her the pistol. "I'm truly sorry."

"Back off, Rebecca. I've got him in my sights!"

Belle stepped in from the kitchen. She was holding Wheeler's Sharps. She could barely lift it to aim at the kid.

"It's all right," Rebecca said. "You don't have to shoot him. I'm inviting Mr. Cimarron to dinner."

"Haskell," the kid said. "That's my real name. James Haskell."

"Mr. Haskell is staying for dinner."

Belle lowered the Sharps. "What happened?"

Slocum waved her off. "Not now."

"Just a minute!" Wheeler cried. "The kid shot me. I won't have him to dinner in my house."

Rebecca smiled at her father. "Patience, isn't that what you always taught me? Tolerance for others."

"And you were lookin' for me with a rifle," Jimmy Haskell said.

Slocum stepped closer to Wheeler. "Look here, if we don't get out of here in a hurry, none of us will have anything for anybody. The sheriff will come calling soon."

The kid frowned. "He's right. He'll hurt Becky."

"No," Slocum said. "He won't hurt her if you'll help me, Kid."

"Me?"

Rebecca touched his arm again. "Mr. Haskell, I'd be glad to have you accompany me to the harvest dance this fall."

Jimmy gazed adoringly at her. "Really?"

"Will you help Mr. Slocum?" she asked.

The kid nodded.

Wheeler scoffed. "Rebecca, you don't have to play up to him. He's a scoundrel."

"He can choose the right path," Rebecca said, looking into

the kid's eyes. "Can't you, Jimmy?"

"The right path," Jimmy muttered.

Slocum looked at him. "Your lookout, Kid."

Jimmy nodded. "Okay, I'm in."

Slocum handed him back his gun.

"Are you crazy?" Wheeler cried.

But Jimmy only holstered the weapon. He kept looking at Rebecca. The kid had a glassy-eyed expression.

"Okay," Slocum said. "Now that we've settled everything—Miss Rebecca, I'll need a couple of your dresses."

Slocum strode toward the stable. The air was still dusty. Shafts of light broke through the evil mist, but it was barely enough to show the way.

The kid came right behind Slocum. He was still stunned, but he seemed steadier now.

They went into the barn.

"What happened to me back there?" the kid asked.

"Love," Slocum replied. "That's why I try to stay away from it. You're a dead man, Jimmy."

Slocum grabbed the black stallion and threw a saddle on it.

The kid's sorrel was also in the barn.

"You think she cares anything about me?" the kid asked.

Slocum glared at Jimmy's mount. "That's my horse!"

"Yeah, I stole it after you shot my hand. You want it back?"

"I'll ride the black for now," Slocum said.

The kid went for the sorrel. "We better clear out."

"Not so fast," Slocum said. "Start stuffing those dresses with straw. Stuff 'em full."

The kid gawked at him. "What?"

"Just do what I say. We've got to hurry. We've got to meet the sheriff before he gets here."

They started to stuff Rebecca's dresses with straw. It had to work. He just hoped the sheriff bought it.

Slocum peered into the dust. He couldn't see anything. The air was too dirty.

"Are you sure this would be the way that the sheriff comes?" Slocum asked.

The kid nodded. "Almost sure of it."

"That damned storm."

The kid leaned forward on the saddle horn. "I ain't never felt this way 'bout a woman. Have you, Slocum?"

"I can't remember."

Jimmy shuddered. "I'm startin' not to like it. Look at me. I'm ridin' against that sheriff."

Slocum shot him a look. "Peters'll find a way to kill you as soon as he has the land, Jimmy. He won't let you live. You're the Cimarron Kid. Sooner or later he has to kill you just to make his reputation bigger."

The kid frowned. "I don't think I'm the Cimarron Kid anymore. I'm Jimmy Haskell now."

Slocum lifted his head. "Listen."

They both heard the horses coming toward them. The kid told Slocum that Cooper's hired guns had thrown in with the sheriff. There would be fourteen men on their tails.

Slocum put the dress-dummy in front of him. "Too late now, Kid. You do the same."

They were using the stuffed dresses to look like women.

Slocum started forward. "Fire a couple of shots when you see them, Kid."

Jimmy drew his gun. "I don't know how I let you get me into this. But one thing, Reb. Me and you still have to fight."

Slocum spurred the black and rode straight for the sheriff's posse.

Sheriff Peters heard the gunshots. He reined back on his mount. The deputies also stopped. Peters had sworn in Cooper's men.

"What is it, Sheriff?"

Peters strained to see in the dust. "I don't—there!"

Slocum and the kid burst by the posse.

"It's the rebel and Wheeler!" someone cried.

Peters grew wide-eyed. He saw the stuffed dresses. "He's got the women with him, too!"

"Wasn't the kid goin' to Wheeler's?"

"They must've kilt him!" Peters cried. "Get 'em. We can't let 'em out of the territory!"

Slocum stopped for a moment and looked back at the posse. The dust stirred higher as Peters chased them. Slocum turned the black forward just as the kid rushed by him on the sorrel.

Slocum caught up with the kid. "They're comin!"

"Lucky for us. Fourteen to two."

They kept on galloping away from the sheriff and his men.

The air seemed to clear a little. Slocum reined back, looking again for the posse.

Peters and the others rode through the dusty cloud that hung over the plain.

Slocum caught up with the kid again.

"How far we gonna run?" the kid asked.

"As far as it takes!" the tall man replied.

20

Slocum rode the black as hard as he could. The stallion headed north in the dust. Jimmy rode behind him on the sorrel. Slocum was surprised that the sorrel could keep up with the black.

Jimmy waved at Slocum.

The tall man reined up. They both looked to the south. It was hard to see with all the dirt in the air.

"Think they're comin'?" the kid asked.

"I don't know. This dust might stop them."

The kid gawked as men rode out of the dust cloud. "They want us, Johnny Reb. We're gonna have to outlast them."

He turned the sorrel and rode north again.

Slocum lingered for a moment, watching the posse. Peters really wanted them. Would he chase them out of the territory?

Slocum reined the black and spurred it into a gallop. He caught the kid after a few moments. They held steady, trying to elude the lawmen behind them.

"We gotta be in Colorado," Jimmy said.

They had stopped on a high, rocky mesa. The air was clear. Slocum could see for miles behind them.

"You think it's Colorado, Slocum?"

"Probably."

His green eyes scanned the horizon. It was the beginning of their third day on the trail. Slocum thought they had finally lost the sheriff.

"We shook him," the kid said.

"I hope so."

Jimmy frowned. "You think he'll go back and hurt Rebecca?"

"Let's hope Belle talked them out of there," Slocum replied. "With any luck, they're on their way to the marshal's office."

Jimmy touched his pistol. "Maybe we should go back."

"Bad idea."

"Why?"

Slocum nodded toward the horizon.

The kid saw the riders. "Shit!"

They mounted up again. Slocum figured they had about five miles on the sheriff. And if Peters had come into Colorado, that meant he probably wasn't going to stop.

"How 'bout Denver?" the kid asked.

Slocum shook his head. "Somewhere east. Maybe Limon."

They started forward. The ground was rocky. It was slow going for a while, but that would also mean slow going for the sheriff.

"We gotta rest these horses," the kid said.

"I know. But we can't rest them now."

The ground leveled off.

They rode hard again. The mounts were holding up, but Slocum knew the kid was right. The horses couldn't run fast forever.

"Four days," the kid said. "You think Peters is still after us?"

"He was yesterday."

Jimmy took off his hat. "He stops when we stop. He knows when we're movin'. He stays behind us with no problem."

"Might have a good tracker with him."

"At least he isn't hurting Rebecca."

Slocum dipped his hands in the trickling creek that ran through the rocks. They had reached the lowlands of the Rockies and the sheriff was still coming. Slocum had figured on the sheriff being a quitter. So much for his figuring.

"Peters is crazy," the kid said.

"No he's not. If either one of us goes to the marshal, he's sunk. So he's not going to stop."

"Would you go to the marshal, Slocum?"

Slocum sighed, looking into the water. "I don't know. If I did, it would only be because of the girl."

The kid's face turned red. "You ain't sweet on her, are you?"

"Not like you," Slocum replied. "Come on, let's keep goin'."

Since the horses were full of water, they had to walk for a while. Slocum kept looking over his shoulder. Maybe they could lose the posse when they reached the mountains.

"Look!" the kid said. "A town."

"Two Buttes," Slocum replied. "We're in Colorado."

"Whatta you think, Reb?"

Slocum sighed. "These horses need oats."

"I could use some sleep."

The town was still in the hot summer air. There were clouds building behind the village. They were dark, like rain clouds.

"Come on," Slocum said. "We might as well give it a try."

They rode slowly toward the town. A sign announced, Two Buttes, Population Not Interested. It was a dirty little place, but there was a general store that sold oats.

"You got any money?" Slocum asked.

The kid took out a handful of gold. "I hit Cooper's strongbox. Damn, he was loaded."

A congenial storekeeper smiled when they entered the general store. "Howdy, gents. Mighty glad to see some customers."

They bought oats and some cartridges.

"You got a watering trough?" the kid asked.

"Out back," the storekeeper replied. "Got rooms, too. There's a shack I'll let you sleep in for free if you spend ten dollars in the store."

The kid slapped two five-dollar gold pieces on the counter. "Load me up, pard. Whiskey, food, a new shirt. Whatever you got."

"There a livery here?" Slocum asked.

"No, but I got some tools out back."

Slocum looked at the kid. "We can rest for a few hours."

The kid nodded. "Not much longer."

The storekeeper studied their faces. "You boys want this stuff in a sack?"

"Everything but the oats and the bullets," Jimmy replied.

The storekeeper put all of the merchandise in a burlap bag. He tied it off and handed it to the kid. Slocum grabbed the oats.

"Ten dollars even," the storekeeper said.

Slocum started out. "We won't be long, sir."

"No," the kid said. "We want to get up to the mining country in a hurry so we can look for work."

"Good luck, boys."

The storekeeper sighed when they were gone. Two of them. Riding together like men on the run. One tall, rugged, the other a smooth-faced kid. They matched the description given by the Oklahoma sheriff.

Normally, the storekeeper would not have bothered, but the Oklahoma sheriff was offering a generous reward.

Thunder sounded overhead. Slocum looked up at the sky. The clouds were continuing to build. He wondered if any of the rain would reach the Oklahoma panhandle.

"You finished with the horses?" the kid asked.

Slocum nodded. He had unsaddled both mounts. They had eaten and watered. They would be ready to run in another couple of hours.

"I think we lost him," the kid offered.

Slocum sighed. "Then it's time to start thinking about doubling back. You have to get word to the marshal."

The kid's face went slack. "Me?"

Slocum glanced sideways at him. "Do it for Rebecca."

"Aw—"

"She's your last chance, Jimmy. If you don't do it, then you're a dead man. Smart-talking pistol punks don't last long in these territories."

"I'll think about it. Maybe after I've slept."

The thunder rolled over the rocky ridges. Light rain started to fall. Then the heavy stuff came down from the heavens. Slocum had to take their mounts inside. The kid dragged their gear into the shack.

"Gonna be crowded," Jimmy said.

Slocum spread out on a hay pile. "Shut up, Kid. Just shut the hell up so I can sleep."

Slocum dreamed of rain beating down on him. Sheets of water fell from the sky. He heard the din on a rooftop above him.

Somebody shook the tall man.

He looked up at the kid. "Shh," Jimmy said. "Somebody's outside."

Slocum rose and drew his Colt. "You sure?"

Jimmy stared through a crack in the wall. "I saw 'em. They're tryin' to surround the place."

"Damn."

"You don't think Peters caught us in this rain, do you?"

"Maybe."

Slocum watched through the rain. There did seem to be shadows moving in the storm. He counted at least five of them in his line of vision.

"We've got to saddle the horses," Slocum said.

"I done it already," the kid replied. "We can run."

Slocum looked at the mounts. "Good work."

"Think we oughta go out shootin'?" the kid asked.

Slocum sighed. "No. Stay low. Don't let them get you. They won't be expecting us to ride out of here."

"We can't get through the door in the saddle."

Slocum put his hand against a rotten timber. "Then we'll just have to go through the wall."

They both climbed onto their mounts. They had to crouch low in the shack. Slocum was holding the stallion's mane.

"Okay, Dobbin. Don't let me down."

He spurred the black. The stallion skittered for a moment. Then it shot forward, bursting out of the shack.

Slocum heard men screaming. He ran toward them on the stallion. Shots rang out, but Slocum was already past them.

He ran north, away from town. He glanced over his shoulder to see that the kid was behind him. They rode hard in the rain.

Slocum knew it would take the sheriff a while to get the posse moving again. They hadn't expected Slocum to run. Peters thought he had trapped him in the shack.

The rain had saved their lives. If the storm hadn't come, they never would've put the horses in the shack. The storm would also wash away their tracks to the north.

Slocum saw the hills ahead of him. The path would be slower through the mountains. How much longer would Peters chase them?

He slowed the black and looked back at the kid.

Jimmy rode up on the sorrel. He had a glassy look in his eyes. His hand also gripped his torso.

Blood poured between Jimmy's fingers. "I'm hit, Reb. One of 'em got me—"

He fell off the sorrel into the mud.

Slocum dismounted and lifted his head. "Kid, how bad is it?"

Jimmy's eyelids fluttered. "Bad, Reb. Looks like we ain't gonna get to have that gunfight after all— I—"

The kid coughed up blood, and then he died.

Slocum let him fall back into the mud. There was nothing else he could do for Jimmy. And the posse was already after him again, galloping through the heart of the storm.

21

Slocum swung into the saddle of the black stallion. He could see Peters and the posse behind him. He spurred the stallion, digging away from the body of the kid.

How the hell had the sheriff reached Two Buttes so quickly? Maybe he had taken a roundabout route, a flatter path from the east. Peters might have been in the town even before Slocum and the kid arrived.

Slocum was beginning to wonder if he was going to get away from the lawman. One of the men with Peters must know the territory pretty well. Slocum just wanted to keep running. He'd take his chances on the trail.

The path began to slope upward. The hills were green. Slocum dismounted when the trail became steeper.

He came down the other side of the hill. The ground was flat enough to ride again. He mounted the black again and headed north.

The rain hit his weary face, but he kept on. If the black could outrun the posse, he could stay alive for a while.

Slocum looked down at the stallion. The animal was thrashing on the ground in pain. It had slipped in a muddy hole. Slocum was pretty sure its front leg was broken.

He turned south, peering into the storm. Now he didn't have a prayer of escaping. Even if he ran on foot, they would still catch him.

The stallion whinnied and beat its neck against the ground.

Slocum took out his Colt. What difference would it make

if the posse heard the pistol? They'd be on him soon enough. He just wanted to put the animal out of its misery.

The report of the pistol died in the rain. Slocum holstered the weapon. The stallion twitched for a few moments before it died.

Slocum sat down on the animal and waited for Peters.

The riders came out of the storm again. At first, Slocum thought they might pass him in the rain, but they turned, encircling him in a ring of mounted gunmen.

Slocum held up his hands to indicate that he was not going to resist. The tall man closed his green eyes. He half-expected them to shoot him right on the spot.

Sheriff Peters galloped up in front of him. "You're the rebel."

Slocum nodded. "Get it over with, Sheriff."

Rifle levers chortled in the rain.

Slocum braced himself.

Peters lifted his hand. "No. Don't shoot him."

Slocum looked up at the lawman. "You gonna offer me a deal?"

The sheriff laughed. "No, I'm gonna take you back to Elkhart to hang."

Peters waved his hand again. Two of the gunmen dismounted. They came forward to take Slocum's guns away. Then they tied the tall man's hands in front of him.

"What about a mount?" asked one of the gunmen.

"We picked up the kid's mount, that sorrel. Let him ride it."

They put Slocum on the sorrel. At least he had his horse back.

It was a long ride back to Elkhart. Slocum thought he might get a chance to escape on the trail. His hopes were heightened when several of the hired guns quit on Peters, announcing that they were going back to Texas. Peters didn't seem to mind. He just paid them off with a handful of five-dollar gold pieces, just like those the kid had stolen from Cooper.

"Take those from Cooper's strongbox?" Slocum asked.

Peters glared at him. "You keep your mouth shut, Reb. I'll put a gag on you, if you don't."

Slocum chortled. "I don't guess you'd want to deal again."

Peters smirked at the tall man. "You ain't exactly in a position to be offerin' deals."

"Try this one, Peters. You turn me loose, I'll get the girl and Wheeler out of your hair. Take 'em away for good."

Peters shook his head. "I can't trust you to do that."

"I don't want to hang."

"But you're goin' to."

Slocum scowled at the lawman. "What about the girl and her father?"

"They're gonna hang, too," the sheriff replied. "Come on, boys. Let's get this ape back to Elkhart."

The posse headed south again, leading their captive through the rain.

22

The river swelled before them, rising in the torrent of rain. It was the Cimarron, Slocum thought. They had been traveling for almost a week in the rain. They had to be close to the panhandle.

Peters spoke with two more of the deputies, who wanted to be paid off so they could quit.

The sheriff paid them in gold coins. Slocum figured the hired guns didn't really know what they had been fighting for. They probably didn't care, as long as they were well paid.

"They're gonna try to cross the river," Peters said.

Slocum watched as the horses waded into the Cimarron. It was wider now, filling both of its natural banks. Slocum wondered how the herds of cattle had fared in the storm. He peered toward the other side of the Cimarron. The riders emerged on the opposite bank. They waved to the sheriff and rode off to the south.

Peters waved to his men. "Go on. I'll come last with the rebel."

The posse waded out into the Cimarron.

Slocum thought he saw his chance.

When the other riders had completed the crossing, Peters took the reins of the sorrel and led Slocum out into the current. Murky water rushed over the sorrel's legs.

Slocum knew that they would shoot at him if he dived into the water by himself, so he jumped toward Peters, knocking the sheriff into the river. Slocum also fell, grabbing Peters as they rolled in the current.

161

A rifle fired from the bank, but it stopped when Slocum and Peters bobbed up together. They both floated downstream. The sheriff started to swim with Slocum hanging on to his neck.

Maybe they would go downstream far enough for Henderson to find them—if Henderson was still there. Maybe he had finally run out like the others.

Slocum went under for a moment. He held his breath. Peters pushed him away. The tall man floated by himself with his hands tied.

He kicked his way to the surface.

Rifles chattered when he broke water. Slugs sliced all around him. He heard Peters screaming before he went under again.

Muddy water stung his eyes. Slocum kicked again. He came up under a tree that had fallen into the river. Something grabbed him from behind.

He was stuck on the tree. Slocum tried to push his head up. But the water was too deep.

Somebody grabbed his shoulder. Slocum floated free. He bobbed up next to the sheriff, who had saved his life.

Peters dragged him toward shore. Suddenly, the posse was all around him. They put guns in his face.

"No!" Peters cried. "Don't kill him. I ain't cheatin' the hangman. Now, get my horse."

Peters turned to slap Slocum's face. "That'll be the last stupid move you ever make, Reb."

After the men retrieved the two mounts, Slocum was put in the saddle again. He felt cold and achy. The move in the river had been a last-ditch effort. He had run out of surprises.

They rode toward Elkhart in the rain.

At least none of the men branched off to the Wheeler place. Slocum prayed that Belle had gotten the Wheelers out of the territory. Even if they couldn't save their ranch, they could still escape with their lives.

They rode into Elkhart in the dark. The rain had not let up. The street was thick with mud.

Peters dragged Slocum through the mire. They tracked mud into the sheriff's office. He pushed Slocum into a chair.

Two rifles were aimed at his head.

"Case I ain't told you, Slocum, you're under arrest."

"Mind tellin' me what for?" the tall man asked.

"Killin' Cooper. You deny it?"

Slocum exhaled. "I killed him. But he was tryin' to kill me first. He had a shotgun on me. It was self-defense."

Peters grinned. "Any witnesses?"

"Wheeler."

"He's an accomplice," the lawman replied. "Put him in the cell."

The two deputies put the tall man behind bars. The door clanked shut. Slocum winced at the sound of the key in the lock. It was a horrible sound. Much worse than the rain that pelted the roof above him.

He lay back on the cot.

It was over for the most part. He would die soon. Peters planned to put a rope around his neck.

In spite of his worries, Slocum managed to close his eyes, falling into a deep, careless sleep.

23

Slocum woke when the keys rattled in the door of the cell. For a moment, the tall man thought he might be going free. But he sat up to see Peters trying the lock in the cell next to his.

Peters slammed the cell door shut. He turned the key and then pulled on the iron door. It was locked tight.

"Gonna put me in that other cell?" Slocum asked.

Peters grinned through the iron bars. "You're stayin' right there till I loop a rope around your neck, Rebel."

Slocum put his head back. He looked up at the ceiling of the cell. There didn't seem to be a way out of this one. He had finally landed in trouble that would kill him.

Peters went out to his desk.

Rain still fell on the roof. Slocum wondered if Wheeler's herd had been washed away. Had Cooper's cattle dispersed in the storm?

A few minutes later, a deputy appeared in front of the cell. "Here's some breakfast, Reb. And some dry clothes."

He slid the tray under the door. The clothes were wedged between the bars. Slocum did not get up right away.

"Well, go on," the deputy said. "Sheriff don't want you catchin' your death, so put on them dry duds."

Slocum sat up. He ate the breakfast and put on the clothes. It didn't matter much to him how it ended. Pneumonia was as good as a hangman's noose. The tall man just went through the motions. He had pretty much given up hope.

He peered into the outer office. The sheriff was talking to his men. When the talk was over, they piled into the street. Only one man was left behind to guard Slocum.

The tall man knew where the sheriff was going, but he couldn't admit it to himself.

He leaned back on the cot again.

The rain kept coming. From drought to flood, he thought. Sometimes nature could be cruel for no good reason.

Lying down in his cell, he could think of all the good opportunities he had missed. He could have run away from Oklahoma at any time, but his obligations had kept him there. For what? To die on a gallows.

He did not move all day.

The rain kept pounding the roof.

Just before dark, the deputy went to get his dinner. Slocum ate stew and bread. He asked the deputy for some whiskey, but the man would only hand him a dipper of water.

Slocum was drinking as the front door opened.

Peters pushed into his office. Two figures moved beside him. They were bound with their hands behind them. The deputies pushed the prisoners toward the empty cell.

Slocum jumped up, grabbing the bars of the cell. "You can't do this, Peters. You can't arrest them!"

Robert Wheeler and his daughter were untied and pushed into the cell next to Slocum.

Rebecca fainted, dropping to the floor.

Wheeler bent over her.

"I shot Cooper!" Slocum cried. "Not them. Don't do it, Peters. You'll regret it."

Wheeler glared at the sheriff. "You savage! Look what you've done to my daughter."

Peters grinned at all of them. "You're under arrest for conspiracy to kill Mr. H. L. Cooper."

"We're entitled to a judge and jury," Wheeler cried.

"I'm the judge and jury," the sheriff replied. "And I just found you guilty. Sentenced to hang by the neck until you're dead. Sleep on that one, Wheeler. You never should've thrown in with the rebel."

Peters and his deputies went out again, leaving one man to guard the prisoners.

Slocum pushed the dipper through the bars. "Here, Wheeler, give her a drink of water."

The rancher took the dipper. "Thank you, Slocum."

"Why didn't you run?" the tall man asked.

"I was stubborn. I didn't think the sheriff would come after us. Belle tried to—"

"Belle!" Slocum cried. "What happened to her?"

"She rode off about a week after you ran away," Wheeler replied. "Said she had given up on us."

Slocum sighed. "That sounds like her. How's the girl?"

Wheeler lifted his daughter onto the crude cot. "I think she's going to be all right. Slocum, do you think Peters is really going to hang my daughter?"

"If she's lucky," Slocum replied, "hangin' is all he'll do to her."

They slept through the rainy night. Rebecca woke at dawn, screaming from a nightmare. Her cries stirred Slocum from a dreamless slumber.

He looked at her through the bars. Rebecca had not done a thing, and Peters was going to hang her. How was he going to get away with it?

The answer came that morning, when the rain stopped. Peters gathered many of the townsfolk in front of his office. He gave them a speech about how Wheeler had tried to take Cooper's ranch. Wheeler and his daughter had hired the rebel to kill Cooper. They had conspired and now they were going to hang.

Someone in the crowd suggested that Wheeler and the girl should get a fair trial.

"Cooper paid all of your wages," Peters said. "Now he's gone. If we're gonna keep this town strong, we got to get rid of the troublemakers."

Another person suggested that they should not hang a woman, no matter what she had done.

Peters replied that all wrongdoers in his town would pay the price, man or woman. He had evidence that Wheeler and the rebel were conspirators. The woman had been in on it, too. They had to pay for their crimes.

Someone stepped to the front of the crowd. "The Wheelers didn't have anything to do with Cooper's death, Sheriff."

It was Thornton, the young blacksmith. Slocum recognized his voice. Thornton started to speak again.

A rifle blast echoed through the air. One of the deputies had shot him. Thornton fell into the mud, dying.

"You killed the smith!" somebody cried.

"He was in on it, too," Peters replied. "Anybody else want to challenge my authority?"

The citizens of Elkhart were not ready to hold another election for the office of sheriff. Peters seemed to know what he was talking about. After all, he was the law in their town.

"Now y'all go on about your business," the sheriff told them.

"When are you gonna hang 'em?" someone asked.

Peters pointed toward the center of town. "As soon as we can build a gallows!"

They started the gallows that afternoon. Slocum heard sawing and hammering in the street. He had heard it before, sometimes for himself. But he had always managed to wiggle out like a worm leaving an apple.

Wheeler and his daughter sat silently in the other cell. They were broken. Rebecca cried most of the time. Slocum hated to see her in such a sorry state.

They did not ask about the kid. Slocum wanted to find a way to tell them that Jimmy had died in their service, but he could not come up with the words. He doubted that they would make much difference, even if he could.

"I don't want to die," Rebecca whimpered.

Her father patted her on the shoulder. "I don't either, honey."

Slocum looked at the ceiling of the cell.

The hammers continued outside.

Saws rasped through wood, making a hellish sound.

By morning, they were testing the trapdoor, making sure it would drop without any trouble. It would betray the dead man's feet. The rope would tighten and his neck would crack.

Peters stared toward the gallows, a glassy look in his eyes. He was thinking of ways to transfer both ranches into his

name. He would own the land before the end of the week.
He had to hang the three prisoners first.

"Sheriff?"

He turned to see one of his deputies. "Yeah?"

"Well, we was just wonderin' who's gonna pay us, now
that Mr. Cooper is dead."

"I will," Peters replied. "You can draw your wages after
the hangin'."

"When will that be, sir?"

"Day after tomorrow."

The man nodded. "I reckon that's okay." He started away.

"Deputy?"

"Yes, sir."

Peters flipped him a five-dollar gold piece. "Spread the
word about this hangin'. I want every tinhorn and sodbuster
in the territory to know we're havin' a necktie party."

"Yes, sir."

Peters took a deep breath. He wanted to finalize his power
in Elkhart. The hanging had to be a big doing. All of the men
and women in his jurisdiction had to be served notice. Peters
was the law along the borderland.

He would be sheriff and landholder. Maybe marshal. He
could even go as far as the territorial governor's office. But
he had to take it slow, careful. And the first step along the
way was to hang the three innocent people in the Elkhart
jail.

The day came for their hanging. Slocum watched from
his cell window as the spectators crowded into the street.
Dawn had come and gone, but no one had called for them
yet.

"He can't do it," Wheeler said. "He can't hang my daughter."

"They haven't brought us breakfast," Slocum replied. "That
means they're—"

The front door opened. Peters strode in. Slocum's heart
began to pound. He wanted to get through it with some guts.
He wasn't going to beg for his life or act like a coward, even
if they did plan to break his neck.

Peters slid trays of food under the cell doors. "Y'all eat up."

"A last meal?" Slocum asked.

Peters laughed. "No, not today. We're gonna hang you tomorrow. Let the crowd get a little bigger."

"It's a regular party," Slocum said sourly.

Wheeler moved toward the iron bars. "Sheriff, let my daughter go free. I promise, I'll sign any papers you want. I'll give you my ranch. Hang me if you will, but let Rebecca go."

"Touchin'," Peters replied. "But we're past that, Wheeler. I don't need your signature on nothin'. I just need you out of my way."

The sheriff left the office again.

Wheeler turned to look at his daughter.

Rebecca smiled. "Be brave, Father. Pray to God. We have to have courage, like Mr. Slocum."

Slocum sighed. He didn't feel so brave. His guts were churning. He could feel the rope around his neck.

No man wanted to die.

But the tall man from Georgia didn't have much choice.

24

Daylight broke over the jailhouse. Slocum had not slept at all that night. The Wheelers had also been awake all night.

"This is it," Wheeler said.

Rebecca patted his hand. "Courage, Father. The good Lord may deliver us yet."

Wheeler looked at the tall man from Georgia. "You think He's going to deliver us, Slocum?"

The front door swung open.

Peters stomped back to the cell room. Slocum saw that the sheriff wasn't carrying any trays. No need to waste breakfast on dead men.

"It's time," Peters said. "The crowd is gettin' impatient. Can't wait any longer."

"Can't disappoint the crowd," Wheeler quipped.

Peters stared at the rancher. "Mighty brave for a condemned man."

Slocum pressed himself against the bars. "Take me first."

Peters frowned. "Yeah?"

"I don't want to watch the girl die," Slocum said. "I haven't asked you for anything. Spare me this one thing."

Peters nodded. "Okay, if that's the way you want it. I was gonna save the woman for last anyways."

Peters opened the cell door and stepped back.

Two deputies rushed in to take Slocum. They tied his hands behind his back and led him into the street. It was cloudy outside. A gloomy day for a hanging.

Slocum started for the gallows.

The spectators yelled at him. Peters had them whipped into a frenzy. They wanted blood. Some of the men had even brought their families.

Slocum suddenly didn't mind dying. He just didn't want to give them a show. If he tried to make a break, the deputies would shoot him. They'd try to wing him, so he could be brought back to the gallows.

Slocum wanted to go out while he was whole and strong. He held his head high for the last walk. The crowd parted to let him pass.

"Kill the scoundrel!"

"Rebel scum!"

"I hear he raped a woman!"

"Murderer!"

The deputies stopped him at the bottom of the gallows. Thirteen steps led up to the platform. Slocum counted them. He counted the loops in the hangman's noose. Thirteen.

Someone pushed him. He started to climb the steps. The rope was thick and rough. He hoped the hangman would lay the knot on the side of his head, so the drop would break his neck. Slocum wanted to die quickly. He didn't want to dangle at the end of the rope with his pecker sticking out. He wanted it to be over in a hurry.

Peters steadied him on the platform. "There's a preacher, cowboy. You want him?"

Slocum shook his head.

"He don't want a preacher!" someone cried.

"Goin' to hell."

"Say howdy to Satan for me."

Peters waved his hand. "Quiet down, all of you. Now, I want you to see what happens to someone who does wrong in my town." He slipped the rope over Slocum's neck.

The tall man was sweating. He could feel the trapdoor underneath him.

Peters positioned the knot behind Slocum's head. "You're gonna die slow, Reb. Gonna kick and strangle a whole lot."

Slocum spat at the sheriff. "Just do it."

"I told you that you would pay," Peters said. "Now it's time." He walked to the edge of the platform.

The crowd cheered.

Sheriff Peters raised his hand.

Slocum kept his eyes open. He was trembling, even if he didn't want to show fear. Sweat dripped into his eyes.

The hangman's hand closed around the trapdoor lever.

"Any last words?" the sheriff asked.

Slocum stared straight ahead, his green eyes focused on the jailhouse.

"Hang him!" someone cried.

Peters started to drop his hand.

Slocum flinched when he heard the shot ring out. He thought the trapdoor had sprung. But he was still standing there, alive on the gallows.

Peters peered to the east. "What the hell?"

He dropped his arm anyway, but the hangman was staring in the direction of the rifle shot.

"Look," someone said. "Riders!"

Slocum turned to look at the men on horseback. Ten of them parted the crowd. They rode toward the gallows.

Peters glared down at them. "What's the meanin' of this?"

A light-haired man in a dirty Stetson drew back his vest. Slocum saw the star on his shirt. He wore the badge of the territorial marshal.

"I'm Marshal McTaggert, territorial government of Oklahoma. Under what authority are you hanging this man?"

"Under my authority," Peters replied. "I'm the sheriff of this town."

McTaggert eyed Slocum. "This man have a fair trial?"

Peters was sweating now. "I—yes, he did."

"No, I didn't," Slocum said. "You ask anybody here. Peters was judge and jury."

The marshal looked into the crowd. "Is that right?"

"Never saw no trial."

"Peters said they was guilty."

"Wasn't no jury; that's for sure."

Slocum almost smiled. The crowd had turned on the sheriff. He didn't have anyone to back him up. Even his deputies seemed to be afraid of the marshal and his men.

McTaggert pointed at Slocum. "Bring him down. And see

if there's any other prisoners in the jailhouse."

Peters scowled at the marshal. "Now hold on. You can't do this."

McTaggert dropped his hand by his side. "Heard some reports of bad doin's out this way. You better—"

Peters had lost his head. He went for his gun. It wasn't even close. The marshal pumped a slug into the sheriff's chest before he had his weapon halfway out of his holster. Peters fell off the gallows into the mud.

The marshal turned, looking for more gunmen. But Peters's deputies had disappeared along with most of the crowd. Nobody wanted to face the territorial marshal. McTaggert had the power to bring them before a judge.

He looked at Slocum again. "Okay, cut him down."

"Marshal! There's two prisoners in the jailhouse. One of them's a woman!"

McTaggert eyed the tall man from Georgia, who was now free of the noose. "You Slocum?" he asked.

Slocum figured it was best to tell the truth. "Yes, sir."

"Come on," the marshal said. "Let's see if we can get this straightened out. We might not have to hang you just yet."

Slocum said that sounded good to him.

After all the stories were told, the marshal shook his head. "I never figgered a man like Cooper would do such things."

"He wanted my land," Robert Wheeler said. "He even had the Cimarron Kid try to kill me."

McTaggert frowned, brushing his bushy yellow moustache. "The kid? He around these parts?"

"Not anymore," Slocum replied. "The posse got him when Peters was on our tail. He caught a slug in the gut."

Rebecca Wheeler lowered her eyes. "I'll pray for his soul."

McTaggert shook his head. "It sounds so farfetched."

Wheeler stiffened indignantly. "Every word I told you is the truth. We barely escaped with our lives. If you hadn't arrived, Peters would have hung us in cold blood."

McTaggert sighed. "What did Peters think he could get out of all this?"

"He wanted to take both ranches," Slocum said. "The kid threw in with him for a while, till he realized that—well, he just didn't want to ride with Peters anymore."

"The kid was in love with me," Rebecca said. "I wish he had lived. He wasn't bad, not really."

McTaggert stood up. "I've heard of land grabbin', but this beats all I've ever seen. Okay, lock 'em up again."

Slocum frowned. "Why?"

"Just till I decide what to do," the marshal said. "Then I'll let you all out again."

Slocum sat on the bunk, hoping that the marshal would see the light. It wasn't long before McTaggert came into the cell room. He unlocked the door to Wheeler's cell. Wheeler and Rebecca were freed.

"Thank you, Marshal," Wheeler said.

Rebecca shook his hand. "Bless you."

"You're free to go," McTaggert told them. "Get back to your ranch. If you're lucky, it'll still be there."

Rebecca looked at Slocum. "What about him?"

"Yes," Wheeler agreed, "we would have been dead long ago if not for Mr. Slocum."

McTaggert took something out of his pocket. "I have to hold him for a while."

"It's a wanted poster," Rebecca said.

"He's wanted for robbery down in Texas," the marshal replied.

Rebecca came closer to the iron bars. "Don't worry, Mr. Slocum. We'll get you out of here."

"No," the tall man replied. "It's no use." Slocum turned away. He didn't want to hurt them again. And the best way to help the Wheelers was to stay away.

Night had fallen over Elkhart. Slocum wondered if the marshal intended to use the gallows the next day. No one had made an effort to tear the platform down. It still stood in the middle of town.

McTaggert lit a lamp in the front room. He moved back toward the cells. Something fluttered into Slocum's cage.

The tall man picked up the poster that offered a fifty dollar reward for his capture. "Gonna cash me in, Marshal?"

The keys turned in the lock. "Come on, Slocum, you're free to go."

Slocum eyed the lawman. "You're not planning to shoot me in the back and then say I was trying to escape, are you?"

"Nope. I ain't Peters. I don't work that way. If I say you're free to go, then you clear out."

Slocum held up the poster. "What about this?"

"You're wanted in Texas," McTaggert replied. "This ain't Texas. Besides, after what you done for the girl and her father, it'd be just plain wrong to hang you."

Slocum wasn't about to disagree with the marshal, even if the tall man figured he hadn't done that much for the Wheelers.

He moved for the open door.

McTaggert stopped him. "Better take this." He handed Slocum a ticket for the stage.

"I had my men bring the coach in early," McTaggert said. "It leaves as soon as you're on it."

"Much obliged, Marshal."

"I suggest you get the hell out of Oklahoma," the marshal warned. "And if you know what's good for you, you won't come back." He stepped out of Slocum's way.

The tall man went past him and then looked back. "One thing, Marshal. Who told you about all the trouble out this way?"

"Woman name of Belle. Came screamin' into my office. Said I better get out here in a hurry. Loud woman. Wouldn't take no for an answer."

Slocum smiled. "That sounds like Belle."

He started for the front door. His guns were on the desk. He picked them up and hurried out. He was still afraid that the marshal's men might shoot him.

But there was no more gunplay.

Slocum hurried toward the stage. He climbed in and the carriage rolled out of Elkhart, taking the tall man west in the darkness.

EPILOGUE

Slocum's stage ticket said he was supposed to go all the way to Wyoming. He didn't mind. It was a free ride and his pockets were empty. He couldn't even buy a plate of stew at the first stage stop.

Still, the ride went smoothly until they reached Coldwater. Slocum saw the sign for the marshal's office. He wondered if there would be any more trouble with the law.

Something happened to complicate matters, but it had nothing to do with the marshal. McTaggert hadn't come back yet. No, it was a woman who surprised Slocum.

He heard her voice outside the carriage. She was complaining to the driver about the way he was handling her trunk. After a few minutes, she climbed into the compartment.

Her eyes grew wide when she saw Slocum. "You!"

"Hello, Belle."

She dived to the other seat, throwing her arms around him. "I never thought I'd see you again, cowboy."

Slocum hugged her back. "You got word to the marshal. Saved the Wheelers. Saved my neck, too."

She laughed. "I'm doing great, Slocum. I have money. A whole purse full."

"Where'd you find a stake?"

"Well, let's just say there are a few men in Coldwater who appreciate the company of a woman."

"That why you're leavin' in the middle of the night?"

Belle shot him a look. "You always were a stinker. I bet

you're hungry. Want some chicken?"

She had a basket full of food for the trip. Said she was going to Denver to see relatives. Things would be good when they got there.

The carriage lurched forward.

Slocum managed to eat even though the coach was bouncing around.

They hit a smooth stretch of trail and the carriage leveled out for a moment. Belle smiled at him. She reached for his crotch.

"Never done it in a stagecoach before," she said.

Slocum tried to protest, but she took his cock out anyway. He grew hard under her touch. Belle sat on him and guided his prick into the wet fold of her snatch. The coach hit a bump. Belle bounced up and down on his cock. She cried out with glee.

Slocum felt the sap rising. He burst inside her. Belle quivered after his release.

Slocum rolled her off his lap.

"That felt so good," she said.

"Thought you was havin' men again, for pay."

She laughed. "Oh, that's not the same. I love you. We're gonna be together for a long time. I just know it." Belle leaned her head on his shoulder.

Slocum put his arm around her.

She talked for a while and then drifted off into slumber. When she woke again, Slocum was gone.

The tall man had taken her purse with him.

After he stole the woman's money, Slocum figured they were square. Belle had cleaned him out once. He had returned the favor.

The tall man walked for a long time before he saw the farmhouse ahead of him on the plain.

He approached slowly with his rifle pointed at the ground.

Someone called from inside the house. "Not another step, pardner."

"I'm lookin' to buy a horse," Slocum replied.

A short, stocky man came out of the house. "Well, why

didn't you say so? You need a saddle, too?"

Slocum nodded. He had left Elkhart so fast that he had not been able to gather his tack. He would have to start all over again. How many times did a drifter have to begin anew?

The stocky man moved toward a corral behind the house. "Been lookin' to sell out. Drought nearly killed me."

"Drought's over," Slocum replied.

The farmer laughed. "Not for me. I can't get any crops up by the end of the month. No, I'm wiped out."

Slocum wondered how Wheeler had done with his cows. But he did not dwell on it. He looked into the corral and chose a tall roan.

"Good one," the farmer said. "I'll get you a saddle."

"How much for both?"

The farmer shrugged. "Hundred dollars?"

Slocum opened the purse he had taken from Belle. He counted more than five hundred dollars. It was mostly in gold.

"The men of Coldwater must have been really good to her."

The farmer frowned. "What?"

"Get the saddle."

"Sure, pardner, whatever you say."

Slocum turned toward the north. Where was he headed now? There was no home for the drifter. Just the open plain, the next turn around the bend.

What kind of luck would he find outside the Oklahoma territory?

He always tried to avoid trouble, but somehow it kept finding him.

The farmer came back with the tack for the horse. "It's a Mexican saddle," he told Slocum. "Worth twice what you're payin' me."

"You agreed to a hundred," Slocum said.

"That I did."

The farmer started to saddle the roan.

Slocum counted out a hundred dollars. He wondered what Belle had thought when she woke up. She sure as hell hadn't expected him to leave her.

"All set, pardner," the farmer called.

Slocum handed him the money.

"Gold," the farmer said with a smile. "I—"

But Slocum didn't hear the rest. He swung into the saddle, guiding the roan to the northwest.

He was going to Colorado again, then on to Wyoming, maybe Montana. He was finally moving north, the way he had planned.

He thought about the lawman's advice. But Slocum didn't take the man's words the wrong way. He didn't mind clearing out of the territory.

Slocum had seen enough of Oklahoma to last him the rest of his life.